A SECOND CHANCE

Jennifer Hetherington had married for money and position, not for love. Widowed whilst still young, she was determined to fulfil the conditions of her husband's will rather than lose her lifestyle to the scheming Hetherington brothers. That was before Mike Manning, a landscaper with an aversion to rich widows, came into her life. A shared interest in creating beautiful houses and gardens brings them close. They are both being given a second chance. Will they take it?

ZELMA FALKINER

♦

A SECOND CHANCE

Complete and Unabridged

LINFORD
Leicester

First published in Great Britain in 2002

First Linford Edition
published 2004

British Library CIP Data

Falkiner, Zelma
    A second chance.—Large print ed.—
Linford romance library
    1. Love stories
    2. Large type books
    I. Title
    823.9'2 [F]

ISBN 1–84395–450–8

Published by
F. A. Thorpe (Publishing)
Anstey, Leicestershire

Set by Words & Graphics Ltd.
Anstey, Leicestershire
Printed and bound in Great Britain by
T. J. International Ltd., Padstow, Cornwall

This book is printed on acid-free paper

1

The Hetherington brothers, formal in their dark, city suits, filled the room with restlessness.

'Well, the farming activities will have to cease, and the sheep sold off. In their place, better to have all cattle, preferably someone else's,' John pronounced.

He picked up a porcelain figurine and examined it.

'A woman couldn't manage Northwood Park on her own the way it is now,' Gregory chipped in.

His interest was concentrated on the bookshelves, and the leather-bound first editions. Standing nearby, Stephen, as always, agreed with his brothers.

'Not women's work,' he said. 'Any hope of getting a cup of tea?'

'I think you might catch Mrs Taylor

in the kitchen, Stephen,' Jennifer Hetherington said pointedly, not moving from her armchair.

'Oh, yes. Right,' Stephen said, sounding surprised, and left the room.

'What's keeping that fool of a solicitor?' John growled, checking his watch with the grandfather clock. 'I have things to do.'

Jennifer said nothing. She wished the reading of the will was over so that her brothers-in-law could go back to the city and leave her in peace to contemplate her future. It wasn't possible just yet. The crowd of mourners out in the garden had to be faced in a show of family unity.

She looked at the two men still in the room. Tall and well-built, they were descendants of a handsome dynasty, if one was to go by the photographs that lined the walls. There was no love lost between the Hetheringtons and herself, and it had nothing to do with looks.

Her body was lithe and well-shaped, her face, whilst not beautiful, always had its admirers. The family was polite, but Jennifer had felt their disapproval from the first time Neil brought her to meet them. It had taken all her resolve not to back out of their engagement there and then.

The years of modelling herself on the languid arrogance of the girls she associated with, trying to win their acceptance, had been hard work. And all to no avail. There was a line, an invisible social barrier, that could never be crossed, and she was an outsider.

'The solicitor's here,' Stephen announced from the doorway. 'Tea's coming up.'

Jennifer put an unnecessary hand to her carefully-coiffured dark hair and smoothed down her black suit as she rose. Such a proper choice, the right outfit for a widow. Proper! That was, or had been, the word for her whole life with Neil. It was the price.

'Warren,' she said, holding out a hand to the newcomer. 'Have you met Neil's brothers? No? John, Gregory,

Stephen, this is Warren Longley, our solicitor.'

The solicitor shook hands with each in turn.

'My condolences to you all. A most unfortunate accident.'

'I expect you're a busy man, too, Warren, so we'll get down to business right away, shall we?' John said, taking charge.

He led Warren to the desk under the window and waved everyone to a chair. His commanding manner reflected his position as the eldest in the family, and a background in the corporate world. But Warren Longley was not one to be hustled. He took his time to unlock his briefcase and remove the solitary, manila folder. From where she sat, Jennifer could read its heading — **Estate of the late Neil William Hetherington**. It was unreal, so terribly final.

'As you are obviously in a hurry to return to the city, I won't read out the will. Enough to say, the terms, in brief,

4

are as follows. The estate has been left in its entirety to Jennifer.'

There was a collective exclamation and a swell of angry muttering from the brothers. The solicitor paused to survey the furious faces, then went on.

'Here is a copy for each of you.'

He passed the papers around. There was silence as the brothers read their copies, then became even louder in their condemnation. Warren Longley raised his voice and continued.

'As you will see, there are suitable endowments to each of you, but there is one proviso. Jennifer forfeits all rights to the property if she re-marries or enters into a de facto relationship. In the case of that happening, it reverts to the surviving members of the Hetherington family.'

This time it was Jennifer who gasped. So Neil intended to rule her life from the grave. She was to go on paying. Surely he hadn't meant to be so cruel. It was John, as usual, who voiced the family's feelings. He came and stood over Jennifer, his face contorted.

'You married him for his money and now you've got it! Well, we'll see about that. We'll fight it!'

He turned his fury on Warren Longley.

'What kind of a solicitor are you to allow this? You must have known she was just a little social climber when you drew up this will. A housekeeper's daughter! Or was it you who suggested to Neil she should get the lot? Is there some arrangement between you two?'

The solicitor remained unperturbed.

'As you've each been mentioned in the will, John, I think you'll find it hard to mount a challenge to have it put aside.'

He closed his case and prepared to leave.

'I'll forget you made the accusations of collusion and improper relations between Jennifer and myself. I'm sure you made them under the stress of the unexpected loss of your brother.'

Jennifer was shocked, but it was still

her house. With the ease of years of practice, she took up her rôle as the hostess.

'I know you can't stay, Warren. Thank you for sparing us this much of your time. I'll see you to the door.'

In the entrance hallway, he turned to her.

'I hope you won't allow the public perception of what is appropriate behaviour for a widow to influence you greatly. When you're over the worst, I hope you'll begin to do the things you want to do.'

She was still grappling with the terms of the will.

'Why did he do it, Warren?' she asked. 'What they say is true. I did marry Neil for his money and position, but I never lied to him about it, and I didn't think he held it against me.'

'I know more about your life than most, Jennifer. Neil confided in me.'

'Then, tell me, is this some kind of revenge? He knew how to make sure I was never going to be happy with someone else.'

'No, it wasn't revenge. He was as sorry as you it hadn't worked out. He admitted to me that you had done a good job but you're still young, and a very attractive woman. It's to be expected you'll marry again. Because this is a valuable property, it might interest men with dubious motives. Not a good basis for a relationship, as you both discovered in your marriage. He wanted to protect you.'

'Protect me? He's saying I wouldn't be able to judge for myself.'

Warren didn't venture an opinion on that, but went on.

'As well, not having had children, the thought of his money going out of the family to some fortune hunter was abhorrent. Nothing I could say would sway him on that. If you marry again, it will have to be to someone who can support you in the style you're accustomed to.'

She gave a short, bitter laugh.

'I wouldn't be likely to make the same mistake again.'

But even as she said it, Jennifer wasn't sure it was the truth. She loved all the privileges that money brought. She enjoyed the position in the community, but it was the gracious home, its valuable contents, the paintings on the walls, even the feel of the Persian carpet hall-runner under her feet, that she loved.

It would take a lot for her to give up Northwood Park. She'd longed to own a place like it from her early childhood, as she ran about in someone else's garden and grounds. What began out of barely-perceived rejection by rich folk grew with her, to become envy and finally determination to enter their world.

Neil's proposal of marriage made that possible. But now it was an appreciation of all things beautiful that held her. And this certainly was a beautiful house.

They reached the front door.

'I know what a shock Neil's death has been but you must think of this as the first day of your new life. And talking of that, please don't cancel on our annual dinner party next month. Judy and I very much want you to come, and everyone there will be most understanding, you'll find.'

'That's very kind of you, Warren. I appreciate it, especially after that unpleasant scene in there,' she said, nodding her head in the direction of the library.

He patted her on the shoulder.

'There are folk out in the garden who genuinely want to speak with you. Go on now, but promise me you'll think about what I've said.'

Her brothers-in-law appeared at the door at the end of the hall. Buoyed by Warren's understanding, she turned and went to meet them.

The awful day was almost over.

'People are waiting, Jennifer,' John reminded.

'Yes, John,' she answered pleasantly,

covering her true feelings with a dutiful face.

★   ★   ★

'There's someone in the garden I haven't seen before. Is it another of your men, Jenny? The gardener?' Margaret Wilson asked during her visit to Northwood Park the following day.

Jennifer turned her attention from the pile of letters on the desk.

'No, Mum. The old gardener retired this winter and his apprentice left to go to the city a week or so ago. I hadn't a chance to get another before this happened. The garden needs attention badly. One of the share farmers kindly mowed the grass at the front and directly outside the dining-room for the funeral, but there's a lot more to cut. Fortunately, the sprinkler system is automatic. I forgot all about watering in the last few days.'

She bent her head and began writing again. Her mother spoke again.

'I think I met him here after the funeral yesterday, but there were so many strange faces, I can't be sure.'

'What does he look like?' Jennifer asked absently.

As she scrawled her name across another thank-you card, she wished her mother would remember not to call her Jenny. It reminded her of the past, their past.

'He's not tall, about our height, of a chunky, solid build. Can't see the colour of his hair. He's wearing a hat. His clothes are good, in fact, you could say he's . . .'

Margaret's sentence tailed off.

It was hopeless trying to concentrate on messages of condolences when her mother clearly was bored. Jennifer got up and joined her at the window. There was no-one in sight.

'He's gone now,' Margaret said.

Jennifer sighed.

'I'd love some tea, Mum. Would you mind making us a pot? We'll use the cups in this sideboard. Oh, and bring some of the cake slices left from yesterday.'

'It's a while since I've seen such a spread. Reminded me of the old days, only I didn't have to bake this time.'

The old days! Her mother was probably glad they were over — long days of back-breaking housework and cooking to support herself and her daughter, in one big house after another. Yet Margaret had never complained, not even when the job turned sour and they had to move on, or when her feckless husband found them and came asking for money.

Jennifer stayed at the window after her mother went happily about her errand. The view of the garden from this room always pleased her. It was intimate, not like the formality of the more public side of the house, with its circular drive and wide expanse of lawn. Because she always spent her mornings here, attending to her mail after Neil went off to supervise the day's work, she felt this was her special

13

garden. She had carefully chosen the colour schemes of the floral displays.

When it was fine, she would throw open the French windows to allow the morning sun to reach right into the room. The two cats, Boots and Smudge, always waited patiently on the steps for her arrival, then came in with a rub against her legs, to purr companionably at her feet.

Jennifer turned from the window now at the sound of her mother's return. She'd had an idea.

'Mum, why don't you come and live with me here?'

Margaret didn't answer immediately. She fussed about with cups and saucers, and slices of lemon, before she sat down and poured from the silver tea-pot.

'Come and have your tea, dear,' she said, at last.

Obediently, almost as if she was a child again, Jennifer joined her mother.

'Didn't you hear me?' she asked.

'Oh, I heard you all right and it's very

nice of you to ask, but no, thank you. You've made a lovely home here, Jenny, but I feel like I'm back in a big house. It makes me nervous, you know, thinking of all that work.'

'Oh, Mum, you'd soon get over that, and once you do, there'll be someone waiting on you, instead of the other way around.'

'I'm very happy in the retirement village. My place is small, but it's all mine. You've done so much already, buying it for me. I realise Neil couldn't have been keen on that at all. He didn't . . . '

She let the idea fade and picked up another cake.

'I'll never understand why you married him. You could've had anyone. There were some very nice boys wanted you, but no, you had to have someone who was above you.'

For once, Margaret got to the point and Jennifer took exception to that. The remark made her sound unlovable.

'What do you mean, above me? I'm

as good as anyone.'

'You weren't one of them, were you? You didn't have the background. There was always that between you.'

'Background? I was reared to their kind of life.'

'Yes, but not born to it. You couldn't accept the difference.'

Remembered hurt rose in Jennifer. How she had hated the not-so-subtle reminders of that difference. When Neil proposed it was a dream come true.

'Anyway, you'll marry again and where would that leave me if the new husband didn't like me either?' her mother went on.

'That won't happen, I promise you,' Jennifer insisted, but Margaret snorted eloquently at that. 'You would be great company for me, Mum.'

Margaret was silent as she poured another cup of tea for them both, then looked her daughter in the face.

'You don't need company. Why, you're not even upset about your husband's death. You didn't love him, but somehow you trapped him into marriage.'

'You're so wrong about that, Mother, and, like everyone else, ready to blame me. I didn't trap him. The fact is, Neil was sure, with real Hetherington sureness, that he could make me love him. When he couldn't, he didn't hesitate to find others who could.'

'Jenny!'

'It's true, Mum.'

Margaret obviously didn't want to hear any more of her daughter's confessions.

'Well, that's behind you now. Perhaps you'll be lucky next time,' she said briskly.

'There'll be no next time.'

'I'll believe that when I see it.'

'I can't marry. If I do, I'll lose this place.'

Margaret seemed past being surprised. She accepted the remark without questioning it.

'And then I'd be looking for another

home anyway. No, I'm staying put in my unit, thank you,' she said firmly.

She stacked the tray with the remains of morning tea and moved toward the door.

'I've remembered where I saw that fellow before,' Margaret said.

'What fellow?'

'The one in the garden. I saw him in the library yesterday, with the boys.'

Jennifer, still engrossed with her own problems, found it hard to follow her mother's conversation.

'The boys?'

'Yes, the Hetherington boys. I went looking for you to ask what you wanted done with something. I've forgotten what.'

'Yes, yes, Mum, you were looking for me,' Jennifer reminded her. 'Was the door closed?'

'I knocked.'

Margaret wandered off. Jennifer smiled spontaneously for the first time in days. She wasn't sure her mother really was vague or if it was her idea of a joke to leave people wondering what she was going to say next.

The telephone on the desk beside her shrilled and put an end to Jennifer's speculation.

'Jennifer Hetherington,' she announced.

'It's Mike Manning, of Secret Gardens, here. I've heard you're looking for help with your garden.'

The voice had a quite distinctive, rich timbre, but a businesslike crispness.

'Perhaps we could help you. I'd like to come to see you and your garden, with a view to outlining our services.'

'I'm rather busy at the moment. Could you give me some idea over the telephone? It could save you a long trip.'

Jennifer decided against adding the words, for nothing.

'That's not possible. I find each garden has its own problems and would involve different approaches. Most country gardens need a complete overhaul.'

'Isn't that a rather dogmatic statement, Mr Manning?' she interrupted.

'You'll find I'm right, Mrs Hethering-ton,' he went on, but with a steely edge to his voice now, 'like a complete overhaul of the sweeping gravel drive and turn-around that belonged to the horse-and-buggy days.'

Jennifer almost dropped the phone. She had forgotten the horse!

'Mr Manning, I'm sure you're wrong but I cannot argue about country gardens just now.'

She slammed down the receiver, and raced through the French windows and out across the garden toward the stables. Jennifer knew her brothers-in-law had been attending to the poor animal in the past three days, but now everyone had left. Was he still locked in his stall? He should have been let out early this morning. She lifted the heavy crossbar on the stable door. Inside, there was silence. She sighed with relief and hurried through the building to the horse paddock beyond.

'Thor!' she called.

The big bay gelding at the far end of

the paddock lifted his head and cantered up to her, stretching his neck over the fence to snuffle around her coat pocket. She put out both arms and embraced him, laying her face against his long nose.

'Oh, you poor thing! I've neglected you. It isn't that I blame you. It wasn't your fault. Neil shouldn't have been racing you through that part of the bush. It's too rocky. You were bound to stumble and throw him.'

At last, after the days of rigid, dry-eyed control, she broke down and the tears came, torrents of tears for the loss of a fine citizen, and an outstanding man-of-the-land, but more than anything, tears for what had never been for them both. The horse stood patiently until she lifted her head, and, with a last slap on the satiny coat, sent him galloping off.

What was it Warren Longley had said? The first day of your new life. Yes, it was but that meant the first day of a new, hard life with responsibility if she was to keep Northwood Park. Could she do it? She knew so little about running an estate.

Pensively, she walked through the gloom of the stables, pushed open the door and stepped out into the sunshine again — and bumped straight into a man about the same height, of stocky build, wearing a hat. Her mother's mystery man!

'Why, Travis, what are you doing here?' she asked, recognising him immediately.

2

'Just being neighbourly,' Travis Reed answered, and stood for a moment, beaming at Jennifer, his brown eyes guileless, before moving to replace the crossbar on the door behind her.

It seemed churlish to question his actions, but the way he had quietly, almost secretly, taken over her garden, made her uneasy. Why hadn't he come to the house and spoken to her first?

'I didn't think I was intruding,' he said, as if he knew what she was thinking. 'I am your nearest neighbour, after all,' he went on.

And he was. His farm had been part of Northwood Park until Neil sliced off the awkward corner of land across the creek and put it up for sale. It had always been difficult to access if the reservoir it fed was at capacity, and the water backed up.

The Reed family purchased the land when Travis graduated from agricultural college and built a modern home for their only son. Because of the creek lying between the two properties, he had not become a regular visitor. Like her, he was in his early thirties, but Jennifer knew very little else about him, except that he had never married.

That was unusual in the district. Most men on the land needed another pair of hands in their early days, and sons to inherit when they finally made good. She felt a twinge of regret for not giving Neil his succession. Would it have made a difference?

'It was very thoughtful of you, Travis. As you can imagine, I've been — '

'Your brother-in-law — ' he said at the same time.

'John?'

'Yes. I was very happy to do what I could when John suggested you might need help.'

That was surprising, totally out of character, considering the venom John

24

expressed toward her during the reading of the will. But what could she say about that to Travis Reed?

'With the water still up, it's a long way round by road for you to come.'

She was feeling decidedly indebted to Travis. His explanation was fair enough but there was something strange about her brother-in-law's request to him. They began to walk back to the house.

'What are you going to do about a gardener, Jennifer?' Travis asked.

She was about to dismiss the question as none of his business when she realised he had already made it his.

'My mother told me she saw you in the house garden,' she said.

He nodded, clearly eager to be of further assistance. They reached the gate. She needed help but she also needed to tactfully draw the line between that and her privacy. She remembered the interrupted telephone call from the man from Secret Gardens. It was a lifeline.

'I'm going to engage a contractor to

look after that. There will be too much for me to do with the day-to-day running of Northwood Park to spare the garden the time.'

'The watering system in the kitchen garden has broken down,' he volunteered. 'I think one or two of the jets may have blocked up.'

Jennifer sighed. She'd never had to worry about such details before.

'I could look at it tomorrow, if you like,' Travis offered, then anticipating her refusal, he added, 'It won't be any trouble.'

What could she do but accept?

'I'll be over in the morning, early,' he promised.

Jennifer watched him disappear round the corner of the house. How had he been able to arrive each day without her knowing? She wondered how long it would be before she'd be able to choke off this neighbourly attention.

★ ★ ★

Jennifer found a parking space for her car a little way down the street from the comfortable Victorian-style home of her solicitor and his family. She'd come here for parties often in the past but always with Neil. Now it felt quite strange to be arriving on her own. The thought of walking into the room, of facing the crowd, and their sympathy, was quite daunting.

She wished her mother had stayed a little longer. It had been company for her, but Margaret hastened her departure when she heard of the party. It wasn't her kind of thing, she said, as she drove off very early the previous morning.

'Rather you than me,' she commented with a laugh, referring to the effort of deciding what to wear and going into the town to have hair and nails done. 'I'm not used to that.'

Until now, Jennifer accepted them as normal activities in a busy social life, but her time had become more and more precious. She was impatient with the hours needed to maintain her appearance.

Without the comforting noises of another person, Northwood Park was overwhelming at first, and she wondered how she could face the future. But after the first hour of emptiness, Mrs Taylor arrived with her husband, Tom, the now-familiar day began, and the question answered itself. Work, that was the future.

Tom had been Neil's right-hand man, and now he became hers. Whatever he thought of a woman for a boss, he didn't allow it to show. There was a job to be done, was his attitude. A routine was established for the day. Mrs Taylor cooked breakfast for the three of them, then discreetly retired to her kitchen whilst the programme for the day was discussed. The morning-room was larger than the estate office, which became Tom's domain. Jennifer valued his knowledge — she would be lost without it and the patient way he shared it with her.

And she valued the friendship of Warren and Judy Longley, her hosts for this evening. Reminding herself of that, she got out of the car and walked toward their home.

'Oh, Jennifer, you came! I'm so glad!' Judy welcomed her at the door with a perfumed embrace. 'You do look well. The outdoor life suits you.'

'It's also murder on hair and hands.'

'Leave your jacket in here, you won't need it,' Judy said, leading the way into a bedroom. 'Now, I might have to abandon you in a moment, but you'll be all right. Travis is here.'

'Pardon?'

'He told Warren he his looking after you,' she explained.

Jennifer was a little irked by that.

'That's an odd thing for him to say. He's been a good neighbour, but I don't expect it to extend to my social life.'

'I'm sorry. Warren thought, if that was the case, he should ask him, to make you feel more comfortable. Was that a mistake?'

'It's all right. Travis was very good those first days after the funeral, before I got a grip on things.'

She didn't add, and every day since! There seemed no end to his goodness.

The doorbell rang.

'There, you're not the last one to arrive. Go on in.'

Judy hurried away, and, left alone, Jennifer's resolve faltered. Behind her, greetings were being exchanged, coats added to the pile in the bedroom. Ahead, the sounds of the party could be heard in full swing in the back garden. She needed more time.

Impulsively, she turned down a passageway that she knew led to the room Judy called her private place. Here, the solicitor's wife found respite from juggling the demands of husband and children and part-time teaching by playing the beautiful grand piano that dominated the room. Jennifer had her hand on the knob and the door half-opened before she realised the music she could hear was not a party CD. She froze. A man was seated at the keyboard, fingers flying, so engrossed in the music he was making he didn't know she was there.

He sat with eyes closed, the strong, masculine face softened by his pleasure in the music. A stray lock of dark hair fell over his forehead as he emphasised a difficult passage. He was good. Jennifer wondered who he was, hope-fully, a new arrival in the town. It could do with an infusion of talent. She stayed hidden quietly in the doorway. The music was steadily building to a climax until, with a final crashing chord, it was over.

There was a moment of stillness. With a theatrical gesture, the man lifted his hands from the keys, threw back his head to shake the hair from his face, and laughed. It was the unaffected laugh of an artiste pleased with his private performance. The sheer vitality of the music and the player, and the glimpse of the unvarnished truth of the man's inner self, touched Jennifer.

Something told her the man wouldn't thank her for witnessing it. Disturbed by a strange sense of intimacy with the stranger, she carefully pulled the door fully closed and retreated down the passageway.

'Oh, there you are, Jennifer. Judy told me you were here, but I couldn't find you anywhere.'

As Travis Reed came toward her, she quelled the blaze of annoyance, reminding herself her neighbour was only trying to be kind.

'Just waylaid for the moment, Travis,' she managed to say, shrugging off the lingering magic of the moment and becoming her social self again. 'It's a perfect night for an out-of-doors function, isn't it?'

'I was meaning to ask you something. I'm having the farrier over tomorrow to shoe my horses. Would you like him to call to check on Thor?'

'But he's not lame, Travis,' she said rather sharply.

'No, and I couldn't see any need for a visit, but he's going to be here and I'm sure he wouldn't mind checking it out. There might be some hidden damage.'

Jennifer could see Travis was determined. She gave in gracefully.

'That's very thoughtful of you, Travis.'

They reached the end of the passageway. Without the slightest awkwardness, she stepped into the family room and was swept up into the party. She allowed her host to detach her from Travis long enough to chide him for his unsubtle ploy.

'You know match-making is a waste of time, Warren. I'm determined to stay at Northwood Park.'

'Just thought it would help you over the first hurdle to have someone familiar.'

'Someone familiar? That sums it up

beautifully. He's become boringly familiar.'

They were still laughing when Travis arrived at her side with a drink.

If Travis expected he would have to escort her all evening, he was wrong. Jennifer was soon greeted by friends. She moved from group to group, catching up with the news. It was as if the guests had tacitly decided not to mention her recent loss. She was glad. It had all been said at the funeral, a month ago now. It was enough that she felt the warmth of their concern.

Passing through a shadowy area of the garden, her attention was caught by a distinctive voice. Where had she heard it before? She paused behind the shrubbery, not consciously meaning to eavesdrop, but intrigued.

'How's business then, Mike?'

'Same as all new ventures, Angus.'

Jennifer knew that would be the head teacher, Angus Kerr.

'It takes a while for your work to

become known. I badly need a showcase commission,' the stranger went on. 'It seems there aren't as many widows with money in the district as I would like.'

'Widows? What do they have to do with landscaping?'

Landscaping! Jennifer realised where she'd heard the voice. This was the caller who'd rang contracting for work in her garden, and with whom she'd disagreed. What was his name, oh, yes, Mike Manning.

Mike Manning laughed.

'Widows! My bread-and-butter, unfortunately. How I hate them! They know a fair bit about gardening but not a darn thing about style or design and landscaping. What's worse, you can't tell them, they're so sure they know everything.'

'You sound as if you've had a personal experience with one that left you scarred for life,' Angus suggested. 'Was it a matter of money or the heart?'

Jennifer imagined a shrug filled the

break in conversation, before Mike Manning went on.

'The last one I rang was particularly prissy and proper. I suggested that her garden might need some attention and she snapped at me and slammed the phone down in my ear. I've been letting her cool off before trying again, as I really need a big contract right now.'

The realisation he was talking about her had Jennifer almost bursting with indignation. She hadn't snapped at him. It had been an emergency that made her hang up on him. She wanted to part the shrubbery and confront him but she could do nothing about what she'd overheard, not without looking a complete fool. But the nerve of the man! Prissy and proper, indeed! What an old-fashioned word, prissy. Proper she'd accept. After all, she'd married into a family intent on keeping up appearances, but prissy! Was she?

Well, she'd intended to get back to him to discuss a contract to look after the garden, but not now. Nothing would persuade her to let him come near the place.

The boom of a brass gong reverberated on the evening air to announce dinner was served on the grass tennis court. Jennifer found Warren had thoughtfully separated her from Travis and seated her between two of the town's long-time residents. She knew them to be cheerful chatterers.

There were quite a few strangers at the long, candle-lit trestle table. Her eyes searched the faces one by one until, at the far end, they found the pianist. With his hair tidied, his tanned face impassive in polite conversation with Warren's secretary, he didn't look the same. This was just another man, quite handsome, but nothing special. Had it been her imagination that he was different? Idly, she wondered how tall he was. The shoulders were broad so he must be over six feet.

Jennifer leaned closer to the woman beside her.

'Who's that seated next to Charlene,

Dorothy?' she asked, trying not to seem overly interested.

If she knew anything about country towns it was that gossip spread like a bushfire and she guessed Dorothy was probably a bit of a gossip-monger.

'Oh, that's Michael Manning, the gardening expert who has opened a new business in town.'

Jennifer heard no more than the name. Mike Manning! The super-arrogant critic of country gardens who wanted to come and inspect her garden, and tell her what was wrong with it, no doubt, and he was the man who patronisingly labelled her as prissy without even meeting her.

She couldn't believe he and the pianist were one and the same person! This Mike Manning couldn't have anything to do with the music she heard. Its magic must have fooled her into thinking he was a sensitive, new-age guy. Just goes to show how wrong you can be, she thought wryly.

The man on her right was saying

something to her.

'I'm sorry, Gerald, what was that?' she asked, trying to collect her wits.

'I said the Shire Council is clamping down further on the by-laws against tree-felling. They insist you have a permit before you remove any from your property, as usual, but now it has to go through the full council meeting for approval. Downright ridiculous, I say.'

Dorothy agreed.

'It's the fault of all those greenies on the council, Gerald,' she said, leaning across in front of Jennifer. 'Won't let you do anything, will they? I wonder if there's anyone willing to stand for election and get them out?'

'Why don't you nominate the new landscape gardener?' Jennifer suggested, then wished she hadn't.

Whatever made her say that? The two residents looked askance.

'But we don't know him!' Gerald spluttered.

'It was just an idea. Surely he would

be against restrictions on the use of chain-saws. He could even sell you a new tree for every one he chopped down.'

'You've heard about him, then?' Dorothy asked.

'No, I haven't. I was only joking,' she explained, wondering what was happening to her. 'What do you mean?'

Dorothy was delighted to tell her horror story to a new listener.

'Kirribilli had him out to inspect the garden and he told them to cut down all the pines along the drive. They've been there for years.'

Ah, another despised horse-and-buggy gravel drive, this time with an avenue of pine trees. Jennifer wanted to laugh but her companions were serious. She looked down the table at the focus of their interest. The flickering light threw shadows across his face. Who was the real Mike Manning?

'But, Dorothy, those pines are probably dead or dying, if they're that old,' she found herself saying.

What was happening to her? Was she becoming a stirrer? And why was she making a case for the insufferable creature? Just because his music-making had moved her? Was she forgetting he hated widows? She needed to change the subject.

The dessert arrived.

'Ah, Summer Pudding! My favourite,' she gushed in her best social manner. 'Haven't the berries been sweet this season?'

★   ★   ★

Jennifer was desperate when Mike Manning rang again. She hadn't forgotten him. How could she? The problem of managing the garden hadn't gone away. There had been no rain and heatwave conditions were quickly baking the countryside. The garden was suffering, too. Tom was becoming more concerned by the day.

'The dams are drying up. The one in

41

the top paddock has become a danger-
ous mudhole. We'll have to take the
stock out of there, and out of the creek
paddock. It's bad, too,' he reported one
morning at breakfast.

'Yes, I pulled one of your sheep out
of the mud on the way home last night,'
Travis added.

The demand for irrigation water in
the drought-stricken country farther
downstream had lowered the level in
the reservoir. It had shrunk back into
itself so far that the land between her
neighbour's place and Northwood Park
had become a sea of mud, a trap for
unwary animals seeking a drink, but not
for Travis, who could carefully negotiate
it on horseback.

Saved from the long road trip
around by the receding water, he
began arriving earlier and earlier each
day. Jennifer felt obliged to ask him to
eat breakfast with her and the Taylors.
He lingered at the table, as if he
belonged, until she and Tom were
forced to leave and do their business

in the little office off the back veranda.

Here, Tom presented a gloomy picture. What was left of the natural feed was being leeched of its goodness by the relentless sun, and with no rain to bring on new grass, decisions had to be made.

'The in-lamb ewes will have to be brought in closer to the homestead and fed a supplementary diet, or they'll become weak, and we'll lose both them and their lambs,' he explained patiently.

'What will we do if all the dams dry up?' Jennifer asked.

'We'll cart water from the council stand-pipe,' he replied. 'Don't look so worried. We've had to do it before, though not for years, thank goodness. Let's look on the bright side. It's a good chance to de-silt the dams, if you're prepared to spend the money.'

'Of course, Tom, that's a good idea.'

He looked at her hesitantly.

'More bad news?' she asked.

'Well, yes. The dam that supplies the

garden should be the first to be done. It's empty already. The pump is sucking mud, blocking the pipes.'

Jennifer was shocked.

'No water for the garden?'

She had been using it as if there was no tomorrow, struggling to keep the thirsty plants alive. Suddenly, tomorrow had come.

'We can't cart water for the garden. Take up too much of the men's time,' Tom said kindly. 'You understand that? Only for the house tanks and the stock.'

'Yes, yes, Tom,' she answered with a heavy heart, stretching out a hand to lift the shrilling telephone, saying, 'Jennifer Hetherington.'

'Mike Manning here, Mrs Hetherington. I was wondering when it would be convenient to call on you.'

3

Jennifer dressed carefully, perversely determined to live up to Mike Manning's expectation of a proper country widow. Her new outdoor life made it almost impossible to keep her hair in its usual immaculate state. For an exasperated moment she was tempted to give up and make a plait, but decided that would be altogether too casual. She tried again to secure it in a sophisticated way, this time with more pins.

As a concession to the heat, she wore her coolest shirt, but made sure it was buttoned right to the top before she opened the front door.

He was tall, as she had guessed at the Longleys' dinner party, the multipocketed chino pants unable to disguise the slim hips. A wide-brimmed hat shaded his eyes. They were blue, of course, cornflower blue. What other colour could they be? Was it a deliberate choice that the cool, short-sleeved shirt he wore was the exact matching shade or just good colour sense?

He stood on the steps, making no move towards entering the house, his attention on the circular turn-around. She could see horse-and-buggy written all over his face. She joined him on the steps.

'I understand we were at the same party recently,' Jennifer said, as an opener to the conversation. 'No-one thought to introduce us. Warren was all apologies afterwards.'

He turned and subjected her to his undisguised scrutiny.

'Frankly, I expected you'd be much older.'

'Why was that?' she asked sharply, surprised by his direct manner.

'Widows usually are.'

Jennifer decided they should get the details out of the way.

'My husband was killed recently in a riding accident,' she said.

There was no need to add he was ten years older than her. Mike Manning was here about the garden. She briefly acknowledged his murmur of sympathy.

'Perhaps we should look at what you came to see,' she suggested, leading the way from the porch to a gate in the garden wall.

He stood aside for her to enter, then followed. It gave her a chance to turn and watch his face when confronted with the garden. He couldn't hide his astonishment.

'You've been to Sissinghurst Castle?'

She nodded, almost running to keep up with him as he strode from one enclosed garden to the next.

'Good, good,' Mike Manning said.

His long legs brushed the low hedges of French lavender, perfuming the air for a moment, before he entered the next section. Jennifer caught up with him at last.

'I fell in love with the Sissinghurst idea of garden rooms,' she explained, 'and colour themes matching the rooms in the house that overlook them,' she added.

She waved an arm toward the bed of delphiniums, and goatsbeards beneath pink roses that grew luxuriantly against a wall outside a bedroom. There was no need to spell it out. The landscaper was obviously impressed.

'I like the vivid blue garden seat. It provides a touch that sharpens the banks of colours,' he said.

'And a backdrop for a black cat that likes to pose,' Jennifer said with a smile, pausing to run a hand down Boots' arching back.

She was enjoying her moment of triumph. Widows with money who knew nothing about style or design! She'd make him eat his words.

It was cooler on the south side of the house, amongst the rhododendrons with their underplanting of hydrangeas, hostas and impatiens. He refused the invitation to sit on the outdoor setting under the trees, but accepted an iced drink left there by Mrs Taylor.

'Did you plan all this?' he asked, and when she nodded, asked, 'Are you professionally trained, by any chance?'

She shook her head, waiting. She wasn't going to prompt a compliment. It had to be freely given.

'Very good,' he said.

Jennifer couldn't help herself.

'Good style and design?' she asked.

He looked at her sharply, and his eyes narrowed. She managed to look innocent.

'Very good,' he repeated.

Content with that, she changed the subject.

'Tom has just told me there's no more water for the garden. The dam has dried up.'

Mike Manning became businesslike.

'You'll have to let the annuals go, of course, but they are nearing the end of their run. You've already mulched, but it needs thickening up to conserve more moisture for the bigger perennials. Keep their roots cool. You'll need to bring in water.'

Jennifer's shoulders slumped at the thought of all that work in an already heavy daily schedule. She was in a no-win situation with this man. Knowing his opinion of widows, she didn't want him here, but needed him badly. Was he a hands-on boss? With luck he wasn't and she wouldn't have to see him again, only his workmen.

'Could you do that? Your firm, I mean. You have the manpower?'

'Yes, we'd take care of that.'

The sun disappeared behind a cloud. She looked up at the darkening sky.

'It does that every afternoon lately, and comes to nothing.'

The futility of the weather made up her mind for her. She'd give him the job, and there would be a bonus — if the work was contracted out, she would no longer be under any obligation to Travis.

'Would you let me have a quotation, please? It has to go through the estate. How soon could you ... your men start?'

50

'Immediately.'

They began the walk towards the front of the house.

'Of course, there's still the matter of the entrance,' he went on.

Was he obsessed?

'I'm not sure I want to do anything about that just now. I have enough on my mind.'

He stood back from the house and eyed it critically.

'It's ugly.'

Jennifer gasped at his boldness.

'Has anyone ever told you you're incredibly rude?'

'Yes, often.'

'It can't be good for business.'

'Surprisingly, it is. People recognise my confidence in my work means I know exactly what I'm doing.'

As if suddenly aware a contract had yet to be signed, he modified his remarks.

'I mean, the front garden and approach is ugly, compared with what you have created.'

Jennifer smiled inwardly. How diplomatically he had saved the day.

'It would enhance the value of the property. You'll be wanting to sell and go to the city, won't you?' he went on.

'Why do you think that?'

'No family. Why would you stay?'

How did he know she had no family? Had he done his homework before he came? That was very thorough. She hoped his work would be the same.

'Because I love the place,' she answered.

'Then, you'd want to change this,' he said, waving his arm.

Mike Manning was actually right. She had wanted to for years, but Neil had been adamant. The conventional view Northwood Park presented to the world was his responsibility, and the back garden just her hobby. He very rarely spent any time in it, dismissive of the cries of delight from visitors. It wasn't men's work.

The landscaper pressed home his advantage.

'What this house needs is a good spring-clean of the shrubbery and a lake to highlight the building itself.'

He was crouching, taking rough sightings.

'Yes, an artificial lake. I'm sure we could get a reflection.'

He strode across the wide expanse of gravel and through the hollow beside the driveway. Following him, Jennifer ventured a word of caution.

'A lake, in a drought?'

He brushed aside her doubts.

'Trust me. I told you, I know what I'm doing. It's a good time to begin excavating, have it ready for the rain.'

'Rain? Well, there's no rush, then,' Jennifer said sarcastically.

He took no notice, already stepping out the distance away from the house, keeping up a commentary as he went.

'I think we could re-route the drive through that area of bush, rather than coming directly from the road. There are no surprises at the moment. The house should be hidden until the visitor comes out of the trees, and suddenly, it's there. More dramatic.'

Jennifer made no attempt to interrupt until she remembered the Longleys' dinner party, and Dorothy's and Gerald's complaints.

'How many trees will have to go?' she ventured.

He looked at her, puzzled.

'None. Why do you ask?'

'You're not a destroyer then?'

'Goodness, no. I'm a tree-lover. In fact, this new entrance I have in mind gives space for the sight of some lovely spotted gums, unappreciated for most of the time. I checked on the way in.'

Jennifer opened her mouth to make a comment about being over-confident but they had reached the first fence. It was not a hindrance to his excitement. He paused only long enough to hold apart the strands of wire and allow her to climb through. They sprang back with a twang after her.

The paddock had been ploughed and harrowed, ready for sowing immediately the first rain fell. The powdery soil, no longer protected by grass, puffed up in little clouds of fine dust with each footfall. Mike Manning was still walking, talking, pointing, waving his arms in the direction of the road. Jennifer temporarily forgot her animosity toward him, her mind full of the pictures his words conjured up. He was right. It would be perfect.

They were in the middle of the paddock when Jennifer felt the first warning sign, a slight stirring of the hot air around them. Mike Manning must have felt it, too. His arms went out quickly to gather her into his embrace, one hand going to the back of her head and forcing her face against his chest. There was scarcely time for a startled yelp before the whirlwind was upon them, the mass of dust, leaves and twigs funnelling violently, with their two bodies at the centre. Although sheltered in his arms, it was still unpleasant. Choking dust invaded her nose and the corners of her mouth. Mike Manning was coughing, too. The force of the wind tore at her clothes and hair, tiny particles of stone hitting her bare skin like pin-pricks.

As suddenly as it had come, the whirlwind moved on. She felt it go and lifted her head to watch it spiral across the dusty paddock and peter out. The hand at the back of her head stayed there, not so urgent now. The knot of hair, so painstakingly pinned up, had become dislodged. Without a murmur of dissent, she allowed Mike Manning to take out and throw away the pins, and fluff the hair that tumbled to her shoulders — to shake out the dust, she told herself.

The man standing so close to her was the music man again, vulnerable yet confident.

'That's better,' he said and reached to undo the top button of her shirt, revealing a point of sun-tanned skin. 'Much better.'

Now she was engulfed by another whirlwind, this time of emotions. She knew she should move away but couldn't. It was as if her standards of behaviour had gone the way of the discarded hairpins. He inclined his head as if to kiss her and Jennifer was shocked at how much she wanted that to happen, but it was not to be. Another cloud of dust enveloped them as Travis drove up in the truck. The sheltering arms were dropped.

'Thought you might like a lift back to the house, Jennifer,' Travis said, leaning from the cabin. 'To clean up.'

She looked down at her filthy clothes, and up at the equally dirty landscaper. His hat had disappeared, and the dark hair was dishevelled. Whatever must Travis think? In her confusion, manners almost deserted her.

'Er . . . Travis . . . er, did you meet Mike Manning at the Longley party? Mike, Travis Reed.'

How easily she said Mike! But it would be silly to be formal after being in his arms, and almost kissed. Whatever had she been thinking of?

The men shook hands, through the open window.

'Would you like to jump in the back, Mike?' Travis asked.

A faint smile caught the corners of Mike Manning's mouth.

'No thanks, mate.'

He helped Jennifer up into the truck cabin and closed the door.

'I want to step out the distances and make notes,' he explained to her. 'I'll fax a quotation for the service tonight and let you have drawings for the proposed re-routing of the driveway as soon as possible.'

The smile had reached his eyes.

'And I need to find my hat.'

He stepped back hurriedly as Travis let out the clutch with a jerk. Jennifer didn't turn to look back. It would be useless. Dust billowed behind the truck, blotting out any rear vision, and the figure of Mike Manning.

'Have you known this fellow long, Jennifer?' Travis asked as they careered across the paddock toward the gate.

'No. Although I saw him at the party, we haven't really met until today.'

In his arms it hadn't seemed that way. What was it about the landscaper that made her forget herself completely?

'You were getting on well for strangers.'

Jennifer looked sharply at Travis. Was this an attempt at humour? That wasn't usually his style, but he was not laughing. He was looking straight ahead, face grim, hands clenched on the steering wheel. He couldn't know that, for once, his presence was welcome. He had saved her from doing something silly. She put up a hand to rein in her loose hair and tried to act unconcerned.

'Are whirly-gigs a sign of drought, Travis? There seems to be an increasing number of them these days.'

At breakfast next morning, Jennifer had no trouble in getting around to telling Travis his help was no longer needed. He gave her an opening immediately on arrival.

'What are Secret Gardens' trucks doing over by the stables?' he asked.

Tom left the room quietly.

'Loading up spoiled hay to mulch the garden. We need to conserve as much moisture as we can, now the dam has dried up.'

'And they are going to do it?'

'Yes. I received a satisfactory quote by fax last night. Mike Manning is certainly very businesslike.'

She busied herself buttering the fresh toast Mrs Taylor brought from the kitchen.

'I've appreciated all the help you've given, Travis, but I imagine you've had to neglect your own place and will be glad to get back to it.'

'You don't know a thing about him!'

The unexpected burst of anger surprised her into looking at him.

'Well, I'll tell you something. Your precious Mike Manning was caught up in some scandal up-state.'

Jennifer wasn't sure what shocked her the most — the accusation or Travis's vehemence. She sat staring at him, knife poised in mid-air.

'And it involved a rich widow!' he added spitefully.

4

Jennifer was dumbfounded. Whatever was going on? No longer the helpful neighbour, Travis had become over-familiar, personal.

'I cannot see what business it is of yours whom I employ,' she said, when she finally found her voice.

His face flushed at the rebuke.

'But it is my business,' he insisted. 'The boys asked me to look after you.'

The mention of the Hetherington brothers inflamed Jennifer. She very much doubted her antagonistic brothers-in-law were concerned enough about her well-being to ask a neighbour to watch over her. It was more than likely Travis had misunderstood them, and taken a casual remark literally.

'So you say. I only have your word for that.'

He opened his mouth to protest but

she silenced him with a severe look.

'And as to Mike Manning's private life, I am not in the least interested. I suggest you save that for the hotel bar or wherever it is you men do your gossiping.'

Annoyed by Travis's cheek, Jennifer got up and stalked from the room, but not in the direction of the Secret Gardens workmen. She'd had enough of men!

Later in the day, guilty feelings overcame her. Travis didn't deserve such a tongue-lashing from her. He had been so helpful, there was no denying it, even if he had been mistaken. He had looked quite surprised at the vehemence of her response. She was surprised by it herself. It wasn't like her to lose her temper. She went looking for him and found him in the stables, grooming Thor.

'I'm sorry I was so hard on you, Travis. You've done what Neil's brothers asked of you and I'm most appreciative, but, you understand, I must manage on my own, not have someone looking after me.'

He replaced the grooming brush on the shelf above the box, and came to stand beside Jennifer.

'But I want to go on looking after you,' he said.

She looked at him sharply, warning bells sounding an alarm. His kindness had become claustrophobic, but was there more to it than being good neighbourly? Did he have a hidden agenda? Was it part of a strategy to make himself indispensable with a view to something more intimate?

Appalled at that thought, she asked herself should she have known this was coming? Her days had been a welter of new experiences, new worries, and romance was the last thing on her mind. But she had heard of divorcees and widows being approached in the first lonely months of their new life, when they were most vulnerable. Was this what Neil had in mind when he wrote his will? The thought of Travis touching her sent a ripple of repugnance through her. She moved away — she couldn't help herself.

What was wrong with her? Looking after her, as he put it, didn't necessarily mean touching her. It needn't come to that. She just had to act firmly and see that it didn't.

Travis was missing from the breakfast table the next morning. Jennifer was glad. She couldn't know for sure if there'd been any truth in her suspicions, probably not, but his absence was welcome. The atmosphere was more relaxed.

Tom was ready to discuss the day's activities.

'When we came in, a water-tanker had arrived.'

'Already?'

'I didn't order it, and don't know what to do with it.'

'I expect it's for the garden, Tom. The contract with Secret Gardens is for worry-free gardening so we don't have to even think about it.'

But think about it she did, or at least about the owner of the business. She'd tried to put Travis's gossip about Mike Manning out of her mind but it wouldn't go. A half-remembered remark made between Mike and Angus Kerr in the garden at the Longleys' party was teasing her memory. There'd been talk about widows but she had been so indignant she couldn't remember what else had been said.

Tom was looking expectantly at her.

'OK, I'll go and see what's happening and tell you at morning break. Did you manage to get in touch with the earth-moving contractor about cleaning out the dried-up dams?' she added.

'Yes. I've booked him. I reckon there'll be a lot of enquiries if the rains don't come soon. What he'll do is move through the district from property to property. He doesn't make any promises as to dates. We'll take our turn.'

Jennifer nodded.

'I can understand that.'

Breakfast over, she helped Mrs Taylor

prepare the last of the tomatoes for bottling. It was almost lunch before she found time to check on the Secret Gardens men. She opened the french windows from the morning-room, stepped out and was shocked into stillness. The colourful display of water-hogging annuals had disappeared! The denuded flower beds lay under a thick covering of mulch.

'It's a bit like tree surgery, when you have to cut off limbs to save the whole tree. Pretty ugly at first,' a voice said behind her.

She started and swung around, ready to be embarrassed.

'I didn't realise you were at North-wood Park today,' she stammered.

It was the first time she'd seen Mike Manning since he almost kissed her.

'There are decisions to be made,' he said, so business-like Jennifer wondered if she'd imagined that was what he'd intended to do. 'It occurred to me we could clean out the dam that supplies water to the garden while we're here.

Save you waiting your turn with the regular man. It won't be doing him out of a job. I hear there's a queue a mile long already. By the time your turn comes many of your stock-water dams will be dried up. He'll still have plenty to do.'

Jennifer became businesslike, too.

'In for a penny, in for a pound,' she said by way of an answer. 'It would keep all the gardening costs separate from the estate, make it easier for Tom to keep the accounts. Makes sense. How soon?'

'The earthmoving equipment is already down at the front gate.'

She raised her eyebrows at that. He shrugged.

'Unfortunately, I don't have a waiting list, being a new business. I'm depending on Northwood Park to establish my reputation.'

'I'm getting special attention, then,' she murmured, and immediately cringed at the thought of how that could be interpreted. 'I mean, I'm lucky.'

The whistle for lunch cut through the

garden. Jennifer was glad of the interruption.

'Ah, lunch. Perhaps you'd care to join me?'

'To discuss the extra cost involved?'

Why did she get the idea he was teasing her?

'Yes, of course. A business lunch.'

Jennifer led the way through the back door into the vestibule.

'I hope you don't mind eating in the morning-room,' she said over her shoulder. 'Mrs Taylor's been busy this morning so it will probably be a scratch meal.'

She opened a cupboard and handed Mike Manning a fresh hand-towel as Mrs Taylor came down the hallway toward her.

'I've set up lunch in the dining-room, Mrs Hetherington.'

Another flush of embarrassment rose up her neck. Whatever would Mike think of this? Would he think it was planned, that she had come into the garden especially to ask him to dine with her? He couldn't know it was a total surprise to her. But how had Mrs Taylor known of his presence? Had she seen him from the kitchen window? Darn! It wasn't the impression Jennifer wanted to give.

'What with Mr John and Travis being here,' Mrs Taylor explained as she caught sight of Mike Manning. 'Shall I set another place?'

'John is here?'

'If you'd rather talk about this later, Jennifer . . . '

She remembered her duty as a hostess.

'No, Mike, you might as well stay.'

'Since you ask me so nicely, OK.'

She wished she could be honest and tell him she felt the need of an ally, but that might reveal too much about her life that wasn't anything to do with him. Their shared laugh gave her confidence. She led the way across the hall to the dining-room.

'Hello, Travis.'

She inclined her head towards her

neighbour and put out a hand to John.

'This is unexpected, John,' she said, and introduced Mike. 'Mike is doing the landscaping at the front and taking care of the back garden.'

Before John Hetherington could make a comment she indicated the table.

'Won't you all sit down?'

Mike was the only one who made the move to pull out her chair. She sat down and passed around the bread basket and then the salad bowl, quite surprised by her calm. She didn't ask her brother-in-law the reason for his visit. She knew he'd get around to it soon enough. There wasn't long to wait. The barest of social niceties over, he came to the point.

'How much are you charging her for the fancy earthworks?' he asked Mike.

'John!' Jennifer exclaimed.

Mike Manning was not thrown by the directness of the question. He returned the belligerent stare coolly.

'I think that is for Jennifer to answer,

if she wishes to.'

Incensed, Jennifer was quick with her reply.

'The details of our contract are a matter between Mike and me.'

John Hetherington took no notice of the warning in her voice.

'I want some answers, Jennifer. You don't think I've given up a day's work and come all this way just to play games, do you?'

'I have no idea why you've come. You'd better tell me. But perhaps it would be a good idea if we discussed it in the library. Travis and Mike need not be involved.'

All appetite gone, she half-rose in her chair. Her brother-in-law showed no sign of getting out of his.

'Luckily Travis alerted me to what is going on.'

'Travis? What has it to do with Travis?'

She sat down heavily.

'Perhaps I should leave.'

'No, Mike, this is my house and I

choose what I do with it, and whom I have as a guest.'

She looked at Travis. He had gone too far this time.

'Travis, I'd like you to go. You are no longer welcome here.'

John Hetherington waved Travis back into his chair.

'He is here as my representative,' he told Jennifer.

'What part of that didn't you understand, John? He is not welcome.'

Jennifer had never challenged any of the brothers before. She was surprised at herself and obviously, so was John Hetherington. His face contorted but before he could say anything, she apologised to Mike.

'I'm sorry you're having put up with this family nonsense.'

Reminded of his audience, her brother-in-law made an effort to control his temper.

'It is not nonsense,' he began in a conciliatory manner. 'You've never had to manage an estate before. It's a big job. I'm here purely as an advisor. You shouldn't be spending money before probate is declared.'

'Warren Longley says . . . '

John Hetherington snorted but Jennifer continued.

'Warren says there is enough money in the trading account. Also, the insurance people paid up promptly, if you must know. That is my money, so it's entirely up to me what I do with it.'

John knew better than to dispute her facts in front of a witness.

'It's the family who is concerned,' he explained to Mike. 'You understand? Now, what kind of experience have you had?'

Jennifer could see where this was going.

'I have complete confidence in Mike's workmanship.'

Her brother-in-law's face told her what he thought of her recommendation. Her efforts didn't seem to be appreciated by Mike Manning, either.

'John obviously has your interests at

heart, Jennifer. He quite rightly is asking for my credentials,' he said, and turned back to the questioner and called his bluff. 'I'd be happy to show them to you if you'd care to meet me in my office.'

He calmly drank the last of his tea and put down his napkin.

'No? Well, that's enough about that. If you'll excuse me, Jennifer, I've work to do,' he said as he rose, pushed in his chair, nodded to the other two men and left the room.

Jennifer was disappointed in him. He hadn't proved as much of an ally as she'd hoped. She supposed it was unfair to expect it. No-one could succeed if they allowed themselves to become involved in the client's family feuds. But she appreciated him being there. John had had to curb his dislike of her in front of the guest. Now Mike was gone she knew she must prepare herself for unpleasantness.

Well, she wasn't going to let John browbeat her. She just had to hold on to the thought that this was her life and she intended to live it her way. If that brought her up against her brother-in-law, so be it. But firstly, she needed to know what had made John so angry about the changes being made to Northwood Park.

'You say you came down here at Travis's request.'

'Yes, Travis rang.'

'Travis had no right.'

'He was concerned.'

'I'm at a loss to know why, since it has nothing to do with him.'

'As your nearest neighbour — '

'If I hear that one more time! Warren is advising me, and, as he was Neil's solicitor, I'm surprised you find it necessary to question that.'

She was fired up by her audacity, and spurred on to question the actions of the stony-faced man opposite her.

'I really don't understand what all the fuss is about. It isn't as if this was your childhood home or that I'm defacing it. This will enhance its appearance.'

John opened his mouth to answer but she cut him off again.

'I see you've finished your lunch. You must be busy. I know I am.'

She rose and held out a hand to her brother-in-law.

'I'm sure you have my best interests at heart,' she lied, as usual — in her circles, it was called being polite. 'Now, if you'll excuse me. You both know the way out.'

John looked flabbergasted as she moved briskly past him, totally ignoring Travis. She was more than a little surprised at herself. Speaking up against the Hetheringtons was something new.

Jennifer was right out the back door before she stopped. She leaned against the door-jamb, shaking a little, dragging in calming breaths of fresh air. A dull roar of heavy machinery disturbed the tranquil garden. Mike Manning wasn't wasting any time! The costing details hadn't been worked out but he was moving into the paddock beyond the garden. She realised he must have used his mobile phone to summon up his workmen.

Jennifer raced along the path to the opening in the hedge that formed a windbreak around the garden. He stood in a cloud of dust directing the driver of the huge earth-moving machine being manoeuvred into position near the dried-up dam. As she reached him, the throbbing engine died down, its ear-muffed driver clambered out of the cabin and began inspecting the site.

'We haven't discussed money,' she protested.

He lifted his goggles up on to his forehead. The blue eyes seemed bluer than ever in the circles of white on the dusty face.

'Well, you are learning!'

He laughed then became matter-of-fact.

'Cliff, here, is an expert. I think he'll tell me it's a straightforward job, no need to break the wall to get at it. When I know that for sure, I'll cost it, draw up the contract and have it to you by fax this evening. We won't begin until you agree to it. I wouldn't swindle you, Jennifer. I'm not like that. Besides, too much hangs on this,' he reassured her before striding off to confer with his workman.

A shiver stirred her skin. The forgotten accusation against Mike made by Travis — had he said it was a scandal or a swindle? She couldn't remember.

5

'Oh, Jennifer! Your hair! You've had it cut!' Judy Longley exclaimed, pausing with the electric kettle in her hand as Jennifer came in the door.

'Do you like it?'

Jennifer pirouetted around her friend's kitchen, the new-style, shorter hair flaring out around her head. It made her feel strangely girlish, quite unlike the proper Mrs Hetherington she'd always been.

'Like it? You look lovely.'

Judy continued with the tea-making, reaching for cups and saucers, and setting them on a tray.

'It's just that I don't have the time to give to keeping it in such formal style any more. It was far too long. It's still longish, but easier to handle.'

'You should've done it years ago. Will you stay to dinner? The kids are away at a camp and Warren promised he'd be home early tonight.'

'Won't I be spoiling a romantic dinner for two?'

Judy laughed.

'That was last night. Two nights in a row might prove too much.'

Jennifer didn't think there was any danger of that. The Longleys were ideally suited.

'Well, thanks, I'd love to. I feel like company. Most nights I'm so tired I make something easy and eat it off a tray on my knee watching the TV news, then fall into bed.'

'Jennifer, is managing Northwood Park too much for you?'

'It's becoming easier in one way as I learn more, but the dry weather is complicating things, making extra work.'

'Tell me what's been happening. Warren said you'd had a visit from John, but naturally he couldn't tell me what about. It was more than just a business matter, wasn't it?'

Jennifer grinned at her friend.

'I got the better of him.'

'You got the better of John Hethering-ton?' Judy said incredulously. 'What's come over you?'

'I feel different.'

'You are different and it's not just the haircut.'

The kettle whistled. Judy got up and made the tea.

'Let's go out in the garden,' she suggested, picking up the tray.

'Yes, let's.'

The friends stepped outside.

'Oh, Judy, this is like an oasis. You should see my poor garden.'

'Yes, yes,' Judy murmured sympathetically. 'But hold on, tell me about your run-in with brother-in-law, John.'

'It seems Travis took it upon himself to ring John when Mike Manning began the work in the gardens,' she began.

'Ah, Mike Manning.'

'Stop it, Judy. Do you want to hear or not? Well, when Mike Manning's men arrived, Travis alerted John, who came rushing down from the city to complain about the changes, and the money being spent. It was so unreasonable. What I do at Northwood Park has nothing to do with him, or Travis. I told them so.'

'Good on you.'

'Trouble is, the family feud began in front of Mike Manning. Don't look like that. He was there on business and it was lunchtime so I had to ask him to stay.'

'Yeah,' Judy drawled, 'of course you did. Just good manners. You're big on good manners.'

Jennifer took no notice of the comment. She was well into the story.

'Mike Manning more or less took John's side, well, he didn't stand up for me. He accepted the family-caring-about-me line, then he left. I had to do my own confronting.'

The talk of Mike Manning reminded Jennifer of Travis's accusation. She wondered if her friend knew anything about Mike's past. Just then the mobile phone on the table shrilled.

'Our peaceful afternoon tea didn't last very long,' Judy said as she lifted the receiver. 'Judy Longley,' she announced. 'Oh, hello, darling.'

As she listened she rolled her eyes.

'Why, of course not. I'll be adding some extra for Jennifer, anyway. Yes, she's here. Perhaps you'd better ask if he would prefer to come another night. I mean, he may not want to mix business with pleasure. OK, see you later then.'

Jennifer wasn't surprised when Judy put the phone down and, with a wicked grin, announced, 'Warren is bringing Mike Manning home to dinner.'

'Does he know I'll be here?'

'Well, no. He'd left the office before Warren rang me.' Almost apologetically, she added, 'It's pure coincidence. The three of us have been getting on like a house on fire. He comes here often to play my piano.'

Jennifer was uneasy. She wasn't sure

she wanted to meet Mike Manning socially, especially after the lunch with her brother-in-law. Although she knew she had been unreasonable expecting him to get involved in a family matter, she was still a little piqued he hadn't taken her side.

'You don't think you should call him on his mobile, give him a chance to back out?'

'Don't be silly.'

Judy looked closely at her friend.

'Unless there's a reason why he should. No? Well, we'll leave it. They'll be along shortly.'

Mike Manning's name hung in the air between them. It reminded Jennifer of Travis's accusation.

'Judy, have you any idea what's in Mike Manning's background? Travis said something about a scandal.'

'Haven't a clue, Jennifer. We take him as we find him. If there's been a scandal, you'd better ask him yourself. Now, how about a walk around the garden? I've been worried about the birds in this dry weather. I found a beautiful bird-bath for them in the city last week. Come and suggest where to put it.'

Jennifer soon found the ideal spot.

'I'd say down at this end of the garden, near the shrubs. They attract the most birds. This far from the house they'll remain wild.'

The friends talked about gardening, admiring the growth of special plants until it was time to go indoors and prepare dinner.

'Jennifer, you're so nervous. It isn't like you. Is there something going on that I should know about? Something you haven't told me?'

'Oh, Judy, of course not. What do you want me to do?'

Judy counted out beans, and left Jennifer to do the vegetables while she checked on the roast beef and began preparing a salad. There was the sound of a car engine, then the deeper, throatier roar of a truck.

'Oh, they're home,' Judy said unnecessarily and hurried forward to greet her husband and his guest as they came in the front door.

Jennifer stood awkwardly in the background, waiting to be noticed. After shaking Judy's hand, Mike Manning turned with a polite smile for a stranger on his face. There was a moment of shocked recognition, and, she was sure, admiration.

'Jennifer!'

He put out his hand. Her host had a moment of surprise, too.

'So, the hairstyle's what you've come to town for,' Warren said, and coming between her and Mike, he dropped a light kiss on her forehead. 'Looks great and smells nice.'

He moved to slip an arm around his wife's waist as she led the way back into the kitchen.

'What have you two been doing, darling?' he asked.

'Talking. I've been picking Jennifer's brains as to where to put the new bird-bath I bought last week.'

She looked back over her shoulder.

'Sorry, Mike, I didn't know you were coming or I'd have asked you.'

'You couldn't have better advice. She has excellent taste.'

Jennifer wondered if he only meant in garden design. Something in his eyes told her not. Colour flamed up her neck. She had been right in fearing social contact with him. It was hard to handle his compliments. Was that only because she was out of practice?

'I appreciate that, coming from a professional,' she managed to say.

Mike took a beer from his host with a murmured thank you but his attention still focused on Jennifer.

'You should consider taking your degree in applied science and horticulture.'

'That sounds a bit of a mouthful, Mike,' Warren said. 'Would all that be necessary to develop Jennifer's talent? She couldn't manage full-time study at the moment.'

'There are diploma courses covering garden design, and landscaping.'

'Hey, you two, how about asking me?' Jennifer cried. 'I mightn't want to become a student at this stage of my life. Going to the city is out of the question at present,' she said firmly.

Not comfortable with the conversation being about her in front of Mike, she decided to change the subject.

'I hear the Picnic Races have been cancelled because the track's too hard, Warren.'

'Yes. The town water restrictions on recreational gardens won't allow the club to turn on the sprinklers,' Warren answered. 'There's a thought, Mike. Talk to the committee about sinking a dam for their own water supply for the future.'

'And landscape that dreadfully boring area around the grandstand,' Judy chipped in, as she leaned over the table to put down the platter of carved beef and vegetables. 'Warren, would you bring the gravy boat from the kitchen, please?'

The conversation became more general, and, as the meal progressed, more light-hearted. Jennifer's wariness of Mike Manning dissipated. Away from the job, he was, in fact, quite charming. She found herself responding to his wry sense of humour, letting down her guard completely. It was a mistake! Late in the evening, the talk had come full circle and Mike Manning was repeating his advice that she go for her degree.

'Yes, why don't you, Jennifer?' Judy urged. 'Then you could make her your partner, Mike.'

It took days, but eventually Jennifer was able to put the embarrassment of her friend's remark behind her. Judy rang the next morning and apologised profusely.

'Mike knows I speak first and think afterwards. He wouldn't be blaming you,' she reassured her.

Jennifer hoped that was true. She

knew she had to erase the memory of his smiling face suddenly closing off in rejection before she met him again.

In the awkward silence that had followed Judy's remark, she'd wanted to explain about the will, assure him he had nothing to fear from her, that she was not a predatory female who would mistake his friendliness for something more. But saying that then would have made it worse. If only he had just laughed and made a joke of the remark! His silence showed a raw nerve had been touched.

It was Warren who had spoken first.

'Oh, Judy,' he said, 'you know that wouldn't suit Jennifer. Anyone for coffee?'

The years of training herself to say and do the right thing sustained Jennifer. She knew how to leave gracefully.

'Not for me, thanks, Warren. My day off is over. Cinderella's pumpkin coach awaits.'

She rose and with a light touch on

her friend's shoulder, gathered up her bag. Mike Manning had risen, too, out of courtesy. He nodded to her, his face a mask of polite nothingness as she left the room.

Now Jennifer dreaded having to meet him again. As it happened, she didn't have to. Whether or not he stayed away deliberately she couldn't know, but his familiar figure was missing from among the workmen in the days immediately following the dinner.

Late one afternoon, Warren rang.

'I don't seem to have the title to Northwood Park,' he said, after they exchanged pleasantries. 'I need to transfer it into your name. Would you bring the document with you the next time you come to town?'

'Certificate of Title? If you don't have it I've no idea where it could be, Warren. I'm sure I gave you everything from Neil's office. But, I'll look again.'

'Did Neil have another safe, somewhere else in the house?'

'No, everything was kept here in the

office, but I haven't had time to explore it fully.'

She put down the telephone and looked around the small office. She guessed it would be easy enough to find but it was just one more thing she had to do. Her mind was occupied with more pressing matters. Today Tom had reported another stock dam had dried up, the water evaporating faster than expected under the relentless sun.

She walked along the veranda and through the darkening house. Upstairs, she looked longingly at the bath and wished she could fill it with steaming hot water and lie there soaking her tired body. Instead, she took a quick shower to conserve water and changed into a clean shirt and trousers before beginning to prepare herself a simple meal.

There was a knock on the back door. It was Travis. Jennifer stifled a sigh. He was the last person she wanted to talk to.

'Oh, hello, Travis,' she said in a controlled voice.

He stepped past her into the kitchen.

'Have I come at a bad time?' he asked, waving a hand in the direction of the food she was preparing.

'I'm just about to eat. Would you like to join me?' she asked politely.

He accepted the invitation and took a seat at the table. They talked of falling market prices, the effect of the deepening drought, while she put together a meal. She hoped Mrs Taylor wouldn't mind her serving up the preserved plums and rice pudding which might just have been intended for lunch the next day.

The meal dragged on, with Jennifer wondering what was the purpose of Travis's visit. He certainly couldn't think he was overly welcome, despite her good manners.

'I think we'll have our coffee on the front veranda,' she said, leading the way to what should have been the cooler side of the house, but it wasn't as the night was oppressively hot.

'Travis, it's been a long day,' she

hinted diplomatically, getting up from her chair and stretching. 'I helped move some cattle and I'm not used to being so long in the saddle.'

'I don't like to see you working so hard,' he said.

Jennifer sighed. How did she get through to him that she didn't appreciate his concern? She was fast losing patience.

'The dry spell has put an enormous strain on all of us, Travis.'

'But you are a woman on her own. It just isn't fair.'

'We don't choose our weather.'

Nor what fate has in store for us, she added to herself, thinking of how she came to be alone. But it was her choice. She'd wanted to stay on at Northwood Park. This was the price.

'You're on your own, so it's harder.'

There was no answer to that, at least, not one he would listen to. To put an end to the one-track conversation, and hopefully send him on his way home, Jennifer picked up the mugs and took them back to the kitchen. Instead of taking the chance to leave, Travis followed her. She bent to stack the dish-washer, closed its door, straightened up and turned, right into Travis. His arms went around her, not to steady her, but to embrace her.

The unexpectedness shocked her. She didn't move, couldn't move. His lips almost savagely covered hers. All her simmering resentment at his interference rose in her. How dare he try this! Life was hard enough without having to deal with amorous neighbours. She threw up both her arms to break his hold, and stepped back, bumping into the sink. There was no escape that way. It gave Travis a momentary advantage. He closed his arms around her again, his mouth seeking hers.

'No! No!' she cried, turning her face from side to side to evade his lips.

'Let me look after you,' he pleaded.

Horrified by that suggestion, and frantic to shake off his unwanted embrace, she found the extra strength to give a final sideways twist of her body that freed her. She stood on the other side of the table from him, her breath coming in short, indignant bursts. She tugged at her clothes, all thoughts of being nice and neighbourly driven from her mind.

'I have no idea why you would think I want to be looked after by you, or anyone else. I just want to be left alone.'

'You wouldn't mind Mike Manning — '

He was venturing into forbidden territory now. White-hot rage consumed her.

'Travis, I want you to go! Now!'

'I'm not going until you promise to marry me.'

'Marry you!'

It was the last straw! The heat, the long, lonely months of hard work to keep Northwood Park going, the Hetherington brothers' antagonism, Travis's obtuseness, all coalesced. Jennifer exploded. She stormed across the room toward him, a clenched fist raised as if to strike him.

At last Travis seemed to understand. He retreated in the face of her rage, fumbling behind him for the door-knob. The door opened and he disappeared into the darkness. When she was sure she'd seen the last of him, Jennifer shakily switched off the kitchen lights and, still fuming, went upstairs.

On the landing, she caught sight of herself in the full-length, wall mirror. Where was the sophisticated Jennifer Hetherington? Gone. And who had taken her place? This wild-eyed virago with hair and clothes in disarray glaring back at her?

How she had changed! She hadn't known she was capable of such anger. What was happening to her?

At least she knew the answer to that. Over the years she had moulded herself into the person she'd wanted to be. Now it was all coming undone. Tears of self-pity stained her cheeks.

6

At Northwood Park all was in readiness for the rain that didn't come. The excavation in front of the house couldn't become an ornamental lake until it did. Only then would Jennifer add the elegant bronze crane statuette she planned to stand among Japanese irises and reeds at the water's edge.

The new approach road from the front gate had reached the house but it needed rain also, to consolidate it. The local dam-sinker was still working his way through the district, and Tom, hopeful of rain with every wind change, grew tired of waiting. He agreed to the Secret Gardens team cleaning out the remaining farm water storages after they de-silted the garden dam.

Now Mike Manning's work was done, there was nothing to keep him. It was goodbye day. He stood at the office door, outlined against the blue of another cloudless sky. As always, Jennifer was pleased to see him.

'Take a seat,' she urged, beckoning him inside.

'All done, except for the weekly watering by my crew.'

Jennifer was sorry this day had come. She'd grown accustomed to having him about the place. Their relationship was easy, despite Judy's gaffe about the two of them becoming partners. When they had met again, he had acted as if a partnership had never been suggested and she convinced herself that it hadn't.

She tried to look business-like, checking the computer screen for any outstanding payments, but couldn't find a reason to delay the farewell any longer. She got up and put out a hand.

'Thank you, Mike.'

Did he hold her hand a little longer than was necessary, or was that her imagination? Perhaps he was sorry it was over, too.

'I'll probably see you around,' she added.

'Yes, probably. It's been great working with you, Jennifer. I hope you'll go ahead with the idea of studying, once the pressure is off. You have a talent.'

The rain came whisper-soft in the early-morning darkness. Quiet though it was, the unusual sound woke Jennifer. For a moment she thought she was still dreaming of the green and orderly Northwood Park, when Neil was alive and in charge, and she didn't have a worry in the world. But there was no partner sleeping beside her.

Unbelieving, she sat up and listened. In the stillness she could hear a faint trickle of water off the roof into the guttering.

It was still raining when the Taylors arrived, Mrs Taylor her usual unsmiling self. She began to prepare breakfast as if there was nothing different about the day, but an unfamiliar grin creased Tom's weather-beaten face.

All morning Jennifer held her breath,

superstitious that if she became too excited it might stop. The radio reported steady rain to the north-west of them and Tom told her that was a hopeful sign. As the day went on, the parched ground greedily soaked up the welcome moisture.

Tom and his men retired to the sheds to carry out maintenance on the machinery and talked with more and more optimism of planting grain crops. The cats came in from the garden and curled up together on the couch in the morning-room. It was their acknowledgement summer was finally over. Even Jennifer's vague mother was caught up in the excitement. Margaret made her daily phone call from the retirement village earlier than usual.

'I'm hearing reports of rain on the radio. Is it raining at Northwood Park, Jenny?' she asked.

Jennifer then decided it was a good day for attending to Warren's request for the Certificate of Title. She systematically searched the office, discovering some Hetherington family photos she hadn't known existed. But there was no sign of the missing document.

'I'm sorry, Warren,' she replied at the end of the day. 'I haven't found it. It must be with the papers you have.'

'Don't worry any further, Jennifer. I'll look through them again. But the good news is the rain. Looks promising, doesn't it?'

'Yes, isn't it great? I'm over the moon.'

'This means you'll have more free time. Come to dinner again soon? We enjoyed having you.'

'Thanks, Warren, I will,' she promised.

As she put down the phone a vivid memory came of her last visit to the Longleys. Mike Manning's pleased look, quickly stifled, when he stepped into the Longley kitchen ahead of Warren, and found her there. She hadn't been able to block that out.

She wondered how he was getting on. Was Secret Gardens prospering? After this rain he'd probably have a rush of work. She hoped so and silently wished him well. A sudden desire to share the excitement flared in her. Surely there could be nothing wrong with that. It was tempting. All she had to do was pick up the phone.

She dialled his mobile. His voice was full of pleasure, unsurprised, almost as if he'd been expecting her to call.

'Hello, stranger,' he said. 'It's looking good, isn't it? Of course, there'll be no run-off for a while. The ground is so dry it'll all soak in. The follow-up rain will be all-important.'

'I know, I know, but . . . '

'You're excited. That's understand-able. I feel the same way myself.'

There was a pause before he went on.

'Have you eaten yet, or made plans for the evening? Why don't we meet and celebrate? We can talk about the rain.'

Jennifer knew she should refuse, that this was as far as she could go with

Mike Manning. Theirs was only a business relationship and a celebratory dinner was not strictly business. But this was also a time for friendship, and she liked to think they were friends, business friends.

'I'd love to. This day is too wonderful to spend . . .'

She almost said alone.

'To let pass without making some sort of an occasion of it,' she finished.

'I agree. It means a lot to us both.'

There was another pause. She could imagine the grin on his face. She'd had one on hers all day.

'Your place or mine?' he asked.

There was no hesitation in her voice. 'Mine.'

'Good. I'll bring the wine. See you about seven.'

Jennifer turned away from the telephone with a flurry of anxious thoughts. Where would they eat? Not the dining-room, too formal, which would set the wrong tone. This was an informal meal for two business friends pleased with the turn the weather had taken. Pleased? The word wasn't good enough. Ecstatic with the turn the weather had taken was more like it.

And what would they eat? Mike was bringing the wine. White or red? She hadn't thought to ask. She looked up at the wall-clock. There wasn't time to attempt to cook anything fancy. It would have to be one of Mrs Taylor's casseroles from the freezer. While it de-frosted in the microwave, she set the kitchen table, but something about the setting looked too everyday. She swept up the cutlery and brought silver from the dining-room. That was more festive but still didn't please her.

Oh, why hadn't she suggested a restaurant? She knew the answer to that. He wouldn't want to be seen in public with her. It wouldn't be good for business, and didn't that go for her, too? The Hetherington brothers would be watching, ready to catch her out.

She decided the table needed an extra touch. There was little hope of finding flowers that had escaped the effects of drought and now the rain, so she grabbed Mrs Taylor's pot of herbs from the window-sill and tried it as the centrepiece. What was wrong with her? Why be so fussy? Of course it looked OK.

Choosing an outfit became complicated, too. The bed was soon covered with discarded clothes.

'I don't have a thing to wear,' she muttered, ignoring the evidence of the bulging wardrobe.

In the end, she settled for black linen pants, a sleeveless red silk top, and casual flats.

Mike Manning had obviously taken care with his dressing, too. She'd become used to seeing him covered by a film of dust as he went about his work at Northwood Park. Tonight he came to the front door looking as fresh as the rain that was still falling. He paused on the steps to look back into the darkness, a wide smile of satisfaction on his face.

'I thought we'd eat in the kitchen if

you don't mind,' Jennifer explained, as she led the way down the hallway. 'Such short notice.'

'Smells great, short notice or not,' he remarked as they entered the kitchen.

'Beef and wine casserole, courtesy of Mrs Taylor's freezer and a microwave,' she said. 'Oh, good, you've brought a bottle of red. Perfect.'

The cork came out with a gentle pop.

'Perfect,' Mike repeated, as he decanted the wine into a carafe.

They both laughed and sat down to eat. The conversation was easy, mostly about the weather, and the effect of the rain on the earthworks. That led into talk about his future job prospects.

'I'm starting on a new job tomorrow, designing another driveway. There's a lot of preparatory work to be done removing an avenue of ancient and mostly very dead pine trees.'

A memory from the Longley party months ago, before she knew him, stirred in Jennifer's mind.

'Would that be at Kirribilli?'

'Yes. How did you know?'

'Oh, I heard it mentioned in conversation. Wasn't there opposition to their removal?'

'Yes, at the time I first made the suggestion. I don't know how these things get around in the country, but the word was out that I was a tree vandal.'

'For the benefit of you city fellows, it's known as the bush telegraph, or at least, it used to be. I wonder what they call it in these days of satellites? Doing the dishes?'

She thought that was pretty clever, but Mike wasn't smiling.

'How about dishing the dirt?'

There was a slight bitterness in his voice. She wondered what had caused that but wasn't about to ask.

'So, could this be the start of something big for you?' she asked, getting back to his work.

His mood changed.

'Actually, Northwood Park was the start of something big for me. People got to hear by the you-know-what that I was working here. It was recommendation in itself. We've been kept busy. Thank you for giving me the chance to show what I could do.'

He lifted his glass in salute, and drank the toast, his eyes luminous over the rim. They seemed more than friendly. Jennifer stared back, unable to think of anything to say to the meaning in them as Mike leaned forward.

'I hear Travis . . . '

'You wouldn't have been recommended by Travis,' she remarked drily, glad to be able to break the spell.

'I was going to say I hear he's still around the place a lot.'

'Not at my request.'

She was too quick with her retort. It alerted him.

'At whose request then?' he asked sharply. 'He's not giving you trouble, is he?'

She shook her head.

'He's just being neighbourly.'

Surely he couldn't know about

Travis's unwelcome proposal. A refusal wasn't something Travis would talk about in the pubs he frequented. She wondered where Mike got his information. As if to answer her, he went on.

'I met Tom in town recently. We had a beer.'

Jennifer didn't like the thought that Tom might be telling tales out of school.

'No need to look like that. I asked Tom if Travis was still around,' Mike explained. 'Why did you turn him down?'

Startled, Jennifer asked, 'How did you know that? Tom doesn't . . . '

She stopped, aware she had given herself away. Was Travis talking around the town after all?

Mike shrugged.

'Pure deduction on my part. Travis acted pretty possessively with you when any other male was about. He also had your brother-in-law's approval. But you don't treat him like someone special.'

Jennifer was reassured. He couldn't

know about the actual proposal. She shrugged, too.

'He's hardly my type,' she said lightly.

The conversation was getting a little too personal for business friends. She got up from the table to take away the used plates and bring over the cheese platter.

'Would you turn down every suitor?' he asked.

If only you knew, Mike Manning! But he didn't. The Longleys wouldn't have told him about the will. Tom didn't know, so it wasn't gossip around the town. The only other people who knew were the Hetherington brothers in the city.

'Certainly,' she replied. 'I'm far too busy.'

She decided to turn the questioning back on him.

'You're not married?'

'No.'

There were other questions she wanted to ask but his manner didn't encourage them. He leaned over and topped up her glass with the last of the wine. A silence settled over them, but it was a companionable silence.

'Do you like piano music?' Mike asked.

'Yes.'

'Do you play?'

'No.'

There had never been enough money for a housekeeper's daughter to have lessons.

'But you have a piano?'

'Yes, the room needed it. I mean, it's a music room. Would you like to try it? It's an age since I've heard it played.'

She led the way out of the kitchen, through the hall to the music room at the front of the house. Mike caressed the grand piano appreciatively.

'A good model, this one.'

He propped up the lid and slid on to the piano stool, flexing his fingers before beginning to play. The music he began with was something vaguely familiar but Jennifer couldn't put a name to the melody. It didn't matter.

She sank into the comfortable couch, and closed her eyes.

'You don't seem surprised.'

His voice came to her above the music.

'Did Judy tell you I play?'

She opened her eyes.

'Yes, but this is not the first time I've heard you.'

He raised an enquiring eyebrow at that.

'You were playing at Judy's the night of the party,' she explained. 'You didn't know I was there.'

His hands stilled and the music died.

'That was private stuff,' he growled, staring at her as if to dare her to make anything of it.

'It was beautiful,' she said softly, remembering the glimpse she'd had of his unguarded self.

Mike seemed satisfied with that. The music began again, the strong brown hands moving confidently over the keys. What was the melody? She sat up.

'What are you playing?'

'You don't know it? It could be your theme song tonight. It's Lady in Red.'

Jennifer was enjoying his teasing manner.

'Or perhaps this is more like you,' he went on, changing the tune.

'What's that? I know it but I can't name it.'

'Can't you guess?'

Jennifer shook her head. She got up from the couch and went to lean across the piano.

'Tell me! Don't be mean.'

The music swamped her as his laughing eyes met hers.

'This really is your song. The Merry Widow.'

Smiling broadly at his joke, he switched to yet another tune, again vaguely familiar.

'*You must remember this*,' he sang the answer to her puzzled look. 'From the film, Casablanca, with Humphrey Bogart and . . . '

'Ingrid Bergman. Of course I know that. Play it again, Sam.'

Jennifer suddenly remembered the words and wished she hadn't admitted knowing the song. She recalled the lyrics, a *kiss is still a kiss* . . . Would he think she was encouraging him? She moved away from the piano abruptly, aware of a change of mood and afraid of where it might lead them.

The music died. Had Mike felt the danger, too? He came up behind her and cupped her shoulders with his palms.

'Goodnight, Jen,' he said softly in her ear.

Smiling, she turned her head to reply. He was closer than she expected. Their faces touched, and his lips travelled lightly across her cheek, to tease the corner of her mouth. Was it just an accidental brushing? It was so fleeting she wondered had she hadn't imagined it was intentional. But she knew she hadn't imagined the tenderness in his voice.

From the door he called, Bogey fashion, 'Here's looking at you, kid!'

116

Jennifer couldn't still her trembling lips enough to reply, before he was gone. She heard the front door click closed, his truck start up.

'Goodnight, Mike,' she managed to say at last, to the empty room.

7

In the busy days that followed the rain, Jennifer thought only fleetingly of Mike Manning, and his kiss. The usual polite thank-you-for-dinner telephone call hadn't come but she accepted such conventional behaviour didn't exist between them. It belonged to the rigid protocol of her other, more formal life.

But she did have a call from Warren Longley, asking her to visit him in his office. When she put in her appearance, he looked quite serious.

'Are you sure Neil hadn't taken out a loan for something?'

Jennifer was surprised by his suggestion that she should know of all Neil's past business dealings.

'I only know what I've learned from you. What are you saying?'

'The Certificate of Title to Northwood Park is missing and I can only think of one answer. He used it as collateral for a loan.'

'But you've gone over the bank statements. What could it be? Nothing new has been bought, not that I know of. If there was, surely it would be showing in the accounts.'

'I don't know, Jennifer, but I'm going to have to find out. There's only one other place any secret transactions — '

'Secret?' she interrupted.

'Did Neil have a lap-top computer?'

'Why, yes, it's in our bedroom.'

'Aha!'

'I haven't got around to doing anything about it. I don't understand them,' she explained. 'I've done well to follow Tom's instructions on the office computer.'

'Would you mind if I call in a firm of city accountants? They're experts at this kind of thing. If there's anything to find, they'll find it.'

'But I don't understand what you're looking for.'

'Don't worry about it.'

He got up from behind his desk and gave her shoulders a reassuring squeeze as he walked her to the door.

'I'll let you know when they're coming.'

He stood with his hand on the door-knob.

'We'll be hoping for good follow-up rains now the ground is soaked. Your new lake should start filling then.'

Jennifer found herself flushing under his kindly gaze. He couldn't possibly know of the last time she'd seen the creator of the new lake, could he? So why was that making her blush?

'Have you thought any more about studying now the pressure of the past few months is off? Mike thinks you have talent.'

She hadn't expected Mike to talk about their dinner together, not even to the Longleys.

'Were you discussing me?' she asked, all prickly.

Warren looked surprised at her sharp tone.

'Of course, we were. You were there. Don't you remember, dinner at our place?'

She did, and she could feel more colour rushing up her neck. She'd almost given herself away. It seemed a good chance to find out more about her landscaper and to divert Warren's attention at the same time.

'Travis mentioned a scandal in connection with Mike. Did he ever tell you what that was?'

Warren smiled.

'Oh, Jennifer, you'll have to ask him about that yourself.'

'But was there a scandal about a rich widow?'

'Are you asking me if he gets involved with rich widows? Again, you'll have to ask him.'

'Don't give me the solicitor-client confidentiality line, Warren. We're better friends than that.'

'Actually, he's not a client.'

'There, so you can tell me.'

'I can't imagine why you're interested. You've worked very hard in the months since Neil died. I shouldn't imagine you're even thinking of throwing it all away.'

'Who said anything about that?'

'You did. It's called body language.'

He touched one of her burning cheeks and laughed as he turned the door knob and let her out into the main office.

It was raining again the morning the man from the city accountants' office came to Northwood Park. Jennifer had been expecting him, standing at her bedroom window looking down the new driveway to where it disappeared into the trees. She carried Neil's lap-top downstairs and set it on the desk in the library, before answering the front door. David Buckley was admiring the view from the steps.

'This is going to look good, once it fills, Mrs Hetherington.'

'Yes, I'm looking forward to that, as you can imagine. Won't you come in? Now, which do you prefer, tea or coffee?'

'Coffee, thank you. Black. The office? Which way?'

'It's not very comfortable.'

'I'm here to do a job,' he reminded her solemnly. 'And I may have to check against the estate records.'

'Well, have a cup of coffee before you get down to business.'

David Buckley was not a man easily distracted by country hospitality.

'The office?' he asked again.

With a sigh she led him through to the side veranda and the office.

'I'll bring you a coffee. Lunch will be at twelve thirty.'

She opened and closed a door, giving him a glimpse of the bathroom. He nodded.

Late in the afternoon, David Buckley announced success. He loaded the lap-top and a pile of papers into his car. It was a miserable evening but Jennifer's offer of a bed for the night was refused.

'No, thank you, Mrs Hetherington. I'm anxious to get back to the city.'

'Did you find what you were looking for?'

The accountant was sticking to the rules.

'Mr Longley will have my report within a day or two,' he answered formally, and professional to the last, he put out a hand to shake hers. 'Goodbye.'

That night, the rain increased. Jennifer lay in the big bed and remembered how the first fall had trickled melodically off the roof into the downpipes outside her window. Now it rushed and gurgled.

The drought is well and truly over, she thought, stretching, settling deeper into the pillows.

The ringing telephone extension on the bedside table shocked her into wakefulness. She squinted at the digital clock. Three thirty! Something must have happened to her mother! She grabbed at the phone.

'Jennifer! It's raining, lots!'

Relief surged through her. She pulled

herself up into a sitting position and smiled in the darkness.

'It hasn't escaped my attention, Mike. It's been going on for days.'

'I mean, it's raining run-off.'

'How can you tell? It's too dark to see,' she teased.

'Not if you get close enough.'

A sudden, ridiculous idea hit her.

'Where are you? Out in the rain?'

'Go to your window.'

Jennifer laid down the phone, threw back the bedclothes and dashed to the window. Parting the curtains, she looked down into the darkness. A torch beam waved in her direction. She picked up the phone again.

'What kind of an idiot are you?' she asked.

He chuckled in her ear.

'Come inside and I'll make coffee,' she suggested.

'No, you come down here and watch our lake filling.'

Our lake! It was a mad thing to be doing, but Jennifer threw on jeans and a

125

jumper, grabbed an all-weather coat from the hallway cloakroom as she passed and opened the front door. Mike Manning was waiting at the foot of the steps, a wide grin on his face. The shoulders of his coat were soaked, and the light caught raindrops dripping from his hat, turning them into glittering crystals.

He took her arm and led her across the driveway, the rain beating a tattoo on their oil-cloth coats.

'Look!' he ordered, sweeping the broad band of light from his torch over the excavation.

What he'd said was true. Tiny, muddy rivulets were coursing down the sides of the earthworks. Jennifer was delighted.

'Oh, Mike, it's filling!' she cried, turning and throwing her arms around his neck in her excitement.

There was a sharp intake of breath, a momentary pause, then both his hands grabbed her by the waist.

'Of course, it is.'

He laughed as he swung her round and round. Her legs left the ground and she was airborne. She tightened her grip and clung to him, squealing delightedly as he whirled her faster and faster, until her body was flying out from his like kids' aeroplanes on a fairground fun-ride. Eventually, he put her down and, still laughing, they ran hand in hand toward the front porch.

Jennifer was aware of one hand still held firmly in his as they climbed the steps. With the other, she pushed back the hood of her coat.

'Come in for a coffee now?' she asked, breathlessly.

He shook his head.

'No, let's go see how the garden dam is doing.'

She looked back into the night. The rain was much heavier.

'Under an umbrella, perhaps?'

'Landscapers don't use them,' he teased.

'I'm no landscaper. I'm only talking about becoming one,' she retorted, slipping inside the house to take a large black umbrella from the hallstand.

She unfurled it and stepped out into the rain. Under its shelter and guided by the beam of his torch, they made their way down the driveway and into the paddock behind the garden.

It occurred to Jennifer that this was what it must be like to share a common goal, to begin a project and see it through from planning stage to fruition, together. Her marriage should have been like that, something shared, not the sterile, polite life she'd lived with Neil. She'd chosen money and position, and all that her ambition had left her with was a beautiful house and the cold comfort of an empty double bed.

There was a glistening pool in the bottom of the garden dam.

'Just imagine that by the end of spring,' Mike said. 'It'll be full of clear water for all your plants next summer. These past months will be forgotten.'

'I don't think I'll ever forget them,' she said, as they crossed the garden to the kitchen door. 'Stay for a coffee now?'

She shook her coat and hung it by the door and kicked off her muddy shoes.

'Are you sure I'm not keeping you up?'

'No, well, yes, you are. But I'm too excited to sleep anyway. Come into the kitchen. It'll be warm there.'

Mike got rid of his coat and hat and bent to unlace his boots, then padded after her in his socks.

'Feel like some breakfast?'

He glanced over her head at the wall clock.

'Good heavens, it's almost five! I'm sorry, Jennifer, I hadn't realised it was so late.'

'Sit down,' Jennifer ordered, moving efficiently between the refrigerator and the stove.

She lit the gas under the frying pan, and dropped in a knob of butter. When it sizzled, she added strips of bacon, and lastly, cracked in the eggs. The toaster popped at just the right time.

'You know how to rustle up breakfast quickly,' he said as she put the plate in front of him.

'Don't sound so surprised. My mother taught me.'

Suddenly Jennifer wanted to tell him who she was, where she came from.

'She was a housekeeper.'

'If she was as good as you then some people were very lucky. You have a way with bacon and eggs.'

'And you have a way with words, Mr Manning,' she retorted, pretending not to be pleased. 'What's hard about bacon and eggs?'

They smiled at each other across the table.

'Coffee? I'm good with that, too,' she teased.

Mike didn't answer immediately. His blue eyes became serious.

'You're a very lovely person, do you know that?'

Jennifer continued to joke.

'Hey, go easy on the compliments,'

she warned. 'I might suspect you of looking for a cooked breakfast every morning.'

She choked off the words as she realised what she had said, and what he might make of it.

'Jennifer, I don't want to become involved with you. I have to make my own way.'

He said it gently enough but Jennifer was already on the defensive.

'Whatever does that mean? If you think I — '

'No, no, I know what you meant, but I think I should tell you that no matter how attractive you are to me, your money stands between us. I don't want a leg-up via a rich widow. I've been called a fortune-hunter before today.'

Jennifer's mind was racing, a jumble of messages clamouring for her attention. Had he actually said she was attractive to him? Did he think she was flirting with him? It was so long since she'd played the man-woman game, she wasn't sure.

But she wasn't free to play that game.

She forced her mind to move on to what else he'd said. A fortunehunter? Was this the scandal Travis had mentioned? Your money stands between us. However he worded it, that was a rebuff.

She took refuge in a change of subject and asked a safer question, one that had come to her often.

'Why are you just starting out in a new business at your age?'

'It's a long story.'

'I'm wide awake,' she reminded him, re-filling his coffee mug. 'I really would like to hear it, if you would care to tell me,' she assured him.

He pushed away his plate and leaned his elbows on the table, the coffee mug between both hands, his gaze holding hers. She returned his scrutiny and, as if satisfied with what he saw, Mike nodded.

'Our family owns a very successful project-building business in South Australia,' he began. 'My father is the principal, my brother runs the materials division. I was in charge of the landscaping division. It was quite extensive. We grew our own trees, shrubs. I suppose you could say what happened was I got too big for my boots. We won the contract to build a large house in the Adelaide Hills for a well-known, wealthy society widow. There was a lot of publicity, and I got to believe it all. She made excuses to consult me in the planning stages, then began asking me to escort her to charity dinners and so forth. I agreed.'

He paused, as if the remembering was difficult. Jennifer imagined how it could all come about. Mike Manning was a good-looking man. She could picture him dressed in formal wear, moving among beautifully gowned women at exclusive, fund-raising affairs.

'At first it was because I couldn't refuse a client, not with the job unfinished, and payment still not made,' he went on. 'But mixing business with pleasure wasn't a good idea and it became impossible for me to separate the two.'

Jennifer's mouth went dry. It was the very thing she'd been trying to avoid, yet what was this that was happening between them? Wasn't it mixing business with pleasure? She took a long gulp of her half-cold coffee. Mike got up and moved restlessly about the kitchen.

'She began to influence my judgement. That in turn reflected on the business. When I eventually came to my senses and called a halt, she turned nasty. Snide remarks about the firm's workmanship soon appeared in the gossip columns. She had newspaper connections. My father's pride in his good name wouldn't allow that. He took her to court, which was a disaster. I had left myself wide open. The firm lost a packet over it, and my reputation was shot to pieces. There was only one thing to do. I had to go.'

Jennifer was shocked.

'Did your father kick you out?'

'Oh, no, I was bad news for the family so I chose to get out, leave the area, and start again far away, here, where I'm not known. Dad is surviving. His reputation is sound among the people who count.'

Mike's face hardened.

'What makes me mad is, she had the money to pay. Dad shouldn't have had to suffer because I was sucked in by a manipulative, society widow.'

So that was why he was dead-set against widows!

'I guess we all get seduced by the glitter of the so-called glamorous life,' Jennifer said.

She knew all about that. She thought of her adolescent fantasy of living in a big house, how it had led her into a respectable but loveless marriage, into a family which never accepted her. But life was full of unexpected twists. It had brought a will that challenged her. She had come through with a new respect for herself and her latent abilities. Mike's decision to leave and succeed on his own would be good for him, too.

'Thank you for telling me,' she said. 'I understand where you're coming from. I want to . . . '

How was she going to say this? Was she presuming to think he needed her reassurance she wasn't another manipulating widow, that he needn't put up barriers between them, because of her husband's will? Why should she tell him that?

She wanted to tell him because they were friends, not for any other reason. And friends shared the secrets of their lives.

'Mike, sit down. I want to tell you something, not about my past, but about my future.'

Now it was her turn to wander the room while she chose the words she needed. She got up and went to the window. It was daylight and the rain had stopped. Everything looked fresh, the plants and bushes washed clean. Across the paddocks beyond the garden, shoots of new grass pushed up the earth. Northwood Park had survived. With this man's help they had come through. She turned to face him.

'Until Neil died I was happy. I had everything I'd ever wanted, a beautiful home, a respected husband, a place in the community. Except for the respected husband, I still have all that. What I'm trying to say is, Mike, you have nothing to fear from me. I'll lose — '

She got no further.

'What's he doing here?' a voice interrupted.

8

Jennifer swung round in surprise as the voice cut across the kitchen. Travis stood in the doorway, his face red with outrage.

'Has he been here all night?' he demanded.

'Travis!' she exclaimed.

'His truck is down at the entrance for every passing motorist to see.'

'It's none of your business, Reed,' Mike said quietly.

Travis stood his ground.

'That's what you think. She won't marry you, you know, not if I have any say in it.'

Jennifer sighed. Mike was right. All this talk about marriage was none of her neighbour's business. Hadn't she made that clear?

'Please, both of you,' she began.

Mike turned to her.

'I'm sorry, Jennifer, I have to go now. I'm due at Kirribilli this morning.'

'Yes, I understand. Thanks for coming by.'

Thanks for coming by! Of all the silly things to say. She wanted to say she wished he hadn't become caught up in her domestic life yet again, but she couldn't. And it was all her fault. She'd allowed herself to dream that she could have his friendship. Was Travis determined to deny her that?

The Taylors had arrived with Travis. They now stood behind him, astonishment on their faces. Was that at seeing Mike in his socks, or at Travis's behaviour? She couldn't tell. Jennifer watched as Mike nodded to them and without another look at Travis, collected his boots and coat at the back door. Soon she caught sight of his tall figure crossing the garden in the early-morning light.

Well, that was that. A new day had begun.

'I've had breakfast, thank you, Mrs T.

What I'd like now is a rest.'

She turned to Travis.

'Was there anything in particular you wanted to see me about? If not, perhaps Tom can fix you up, because frankly, I've had enough of you.'

She strode out of the room.

'Jennifer!'

Travis followed her into the hallway.

Gritting her teeth, she turned back to face him.

'What is it now, Travis?'

'Don't be angry with me. I have to look after my own interests.'

'Why shouldn't I be angry with you? You embarrassed me in front of a business associate. I wish you'd get it into your head your so-called interests have nothing to do with me.'

'But that's not true. They said they'd make it worth my while if I made it my interest.'

In spite of her anger with her neighbour, Jennifer was intrigued.

'Whatever are you talking about?'

'John offered to pay me . . . '

'What?

She was almost shouting. The Taylors could probably hear her in the kitchen. Lowering her voice, she grabbed Travis by the arm.

'Here, come into the library.'

She ushered him through the door and closed it after them.

'Now, start again.'

'On the day of the funeral, John and his brothers made me this offer.'

'Yes, yes, they asked you to look after me. I know that. So they were going to pay you to look after me, is that what you're saying?'

'No, pay me to marry you.'

Jennifer couldn't believe what she was hearing.

'Marry me! You mean to marry me for money?'

He nodded. It fuelled her anger.

'Am I goods, to be bargained for? How much? On second thoughts, I don't want to know my price. It would probably shock me even further. Oh, Travis, how could you even consider it?'

'I'm desperate. My farm's in real trouble. Last year I bought some expensive stock for breeding which cleaned me out of ready cash. The drought has meant buying feed. Well, they knew I was needing financial help. I thought it was a way out.'

At least this explained his persistence since the day of the funeral, why he was always under foot, why nothing seemed to get through to him. The brothers were offering him money. She wondered if they had told him why. Did he ask? Or was his need so great he hadn't wanted to know and why would they do that? The questions were unending, but with a sinking heart, she knew the answer to them all. The Hetherington brothers wanted Northwood Park.

The depth of their dislike of her and the deceit they were prepared to go to in order to achieve their goal, the breaking of the will, astounded her. She wasn't capable of such ruthlessness and found it hard to understand it in others, and poor Travis was merely a pawn in their game. She was sure they hadn't told him that whatever they paid him it was nothing to what they stood to gain. Suddenly she felt sorry for him. He was just a victim.

'Travis, there's no way — '

'I know,' he said and gave her a crooked smile. 'It wasn't only for the money, you know. I've always — '

Jennifer didn't want to hear that.

'Why haven't you married?' she broke in.

'My mother always found fault with the girls I brought home. Wait for Miss Right, she used to say. I waited too long.'

'I'm really sorry about this, Travis. You were a great help to me when I needed someone, but it's over, you understand?'

'Don't you worry about it, Jennifer. I'll pull through. This rain will help. Stock prices will go up.'

'Good,' Jennifer said, her mind already shifting to the Hetherington brothers.

What was she going to do about this revelation? What could she do? Probably nothing except let them know what she thought of their rotten scheme. Somewhere in the house the phone was ringing, then it stopped. After a while, Mrs Taylor poked her head around the door.

'Warren Longley wants to speak to you, Mrs Hetherington.'

'Warren?'

She looked at the grandfather clock.

'At this hour of the morning? I'll take it in my bedroom, Mrs Taylor. Excuse me, Travis,' she said and hurried up the stairs.

'This is an early start for you, Warren,' she said into the phone. 'Are you keeping farmers' hours these days?'

'Ah, Jennifer, I'm glad I caught you.'

'As it happens, Warren, I was going to ring you later. I have the most astonishing thing to tell you. You'll never believe what the brothers . . . '

The words were tumbling over themselves.

'I'm coming to dinner with you and Judy tomorrow night. We arranged it last week, and — '

'Jennifer, I need to see you urgently about another matter.'

His formal tone stopped her rush of words.

'I'm in court this morning but could you come into my office this afternoon? I have a free appointment about four o'clock.'

Jennifer was suddenly aware of her lack of sleep. The thought of driving to town and discussing business was too much.

'But I'm coming to dinner tomorrow.'

'Today, if you wouldn't mind,' he insisted.

Jennifer supposed it was something legal that had to be finalised.

'OK, OK, I'll be seeing you twice in two days, that'll be good. Four o'clock, then.'

After all the excitement of the night and Travis's revelations, Jennifer didn't think she would be able to sleep, but the moment she put her head down on the pillow she felt herself drifting off. She didn't remember a thing until Mrs Taylor called her for lunch.

The atmosphere in the kitchen was strained. Mrs Taylor was her usual dour self as she placed the roast leg of lamb in front of Tom, but he sat there without taking up the carvers. Jennifer wondered what had wiped the smile off his face. There was nothing to worry about now it had rained. Was it a disagreement between them? She hoped it wasn't disapproval of the shoeless Mike or anything to do with the row with Travis.

'Is something wrong?' she asked.

Tom glanced at his wife then back to Jennifer.

'There's been an accident.'

Her heart gave a lurch.

'To one of the men?'

'No, no, not to our men.'

Her anxiety fell to a reasonable level but the Taylors' faces remained serious.

She realised something more was expected of her.

'To whom, Tom?'

He looked at his wife again before answering.

'Over at Kirribilli.'

For a moment, Jennifer didn't make the connection. Reassured of the safety of her men, her mind had turned to her coming visit to Warren and what she had to tell him. She grasped a chair and pulled it out.

'I'm sorry to hear that. Is it someone you know?'

'Yes.'

Tom seemed to be having difficulty coming out with the news.

'Harry came that way delivering a spare part for the tractor. He said they had started removing those dead pine trees that line the driveway.'

The dead pine trees at Kirribilli! Jennifer felt a cold dread clutch at her heart. Mike and his men were to start there this morning.

'Who has been hurt?' she asked,

afraid of the answer.

'Harry didn't know. He just knew a tree had fallen on someone.'

Someone? What if it was Mike who had been hurt? Jennifer loosened her grip on the back of the chair. There was no question of what she would do.

'I'll go,' she said.

Mrs Taylor spoke at last.

'You can't go without something to eat.'

She dismissed Mrs Taylor's fussing with a wave of her hand. There wasn't time to eat. She looked around for her car keys and handbag.

'At least have a cup of tea before you go, Mrs Hetherington,' Mrs Taylor insisted, already pouring it.

Tom backed up his wife.

'Go on, lass, you'll be no good without something.'

'There isn't time.'

'Yes, there is. Drink your tea while I make you a couple of sandwiches to eat on the way,' Mrs Taylor said, buttering bread.

Jennifer would never have pictured herself eating a sandwich as she drove. Certainly the idea wouldn't have appealed to the old Jennifer, but she was a different woman now, and this was an emergency. Anything was possible.

Tom carved off slices of lamb and laid them on the home-made bread and closed each sandwich, trimming the crusts. Working as a team, it only took them a few minutes. Mrs Taylor permitted herself a little smile of encouragement as she handed over the foil-wrapped parcel.

'It might be good news,' she said.

'Of course, it might,' Jennifer replied, touched by her concern. 'It could be a mistake.'

But Jennifer felt less confident as she steered the car down Mike's new road to the property entrance, and turned westwards towards Kirribilli. Her mind kept coming up with dreadful scenarios. He'd been up all night and was probably tired. It was easy to become careless with machinery. She reminded herself he didn't normally use the machinery, his men did that.

Another worry took hold. His reflexes wouldn't be as good as usual if he was tired. A falling tree could have caught him unawares. A sudden image rose of him spreadeagled on the ground under the branches, the lithe body lying still, pine needles covering the dark hair.

She choked back a sob and gripped the steering wheel more tightly. Couldn't she go any faster without breaking the law? She increased the pressure on the accelerator. At last came the signpost she was looking for! The landmark avenue of pine trees wasn't long in appearing after that. She slowed, turned in and rattled over the cattle grid and drove between the ragged line of trees.

The Secret Gardens team had begun to remove the trees closer to the house. A cluster of trucks and machinery gathered in the forecourt. Her eyes eagerly looked for Mike's familiar truck. It was there, but even as she rejoiced in that discovery she realised it didn't mean he was there. If he was injured an ambulance would have taken him away by now.

Jennifer flung open the car door when she parked and hurried across the gravel toward the group of ear-muffed workmen wielding screaming chainsaws on a huge, old pine that lay on the ground. There was no sign of Mike.

'Mike?' she shouted to the nearest workman.

He silenced his equipment and removed his protective ear-muffs.

'Mike?' she repeated.

He grinned and pointed toward the house, then pulled the starter rope and the machine roared into action again. The noise tore through Jennifer's head. It was work as usual. Did that mean Mike was all right? It must. The man had smiled.

She suddenly felt weak with relief and, she guessed, lack of food. Tom had been right. She should have eaten. She wanted to leave now, before Mike learned of her mad rush, because that was what it was. Deserted by common-sense and acting purely on emotion, she'd made a mindless dash across country to find him. She felt sillier with each moment. But could her legs carry her back to her car?

She picked her way through scattered pine cones, the heels of her town shoes sinking into the soft ground. Her mind registered the house for the first time. It was not new, built in the colonial style. She could see why the half-dead pines had to go. They overpowered it. She wondered what trees Mike had chosen as replacement. An avenue of flowering gums would look great, perhaps with oyster-grey trunks that picked up the colour of the stone. She smiled to herself. She was becoming a land-scaper!

Jennifer reached the car and flopped into the front seat. She leaned forward and laid her head on the steering wheel and let go, lost in the world of noise and delayed shock.

'Why, hello!'

The greeting was shouted through the open door. Jennifer jerked back into a sitting position at Mike's voice.

'What are you doing here?' he asked.

She looked blankly at him.

'Hey, you've been crying,' he exclaimed.

She put up a hand and was surprised to feel tears on her cheeks. He closed the door and moved quickly around the car and got in the passenger side.

'Wind up your window,' he ordered gently

Almost trance-like she did as she was told. The noise died away.

'Now tell me, what's up?'

'We heard someone was hurt in an accident with a tree, and I . . . '

'You came out here to check?'

She nodded.

'And why are you crying?'

A little sense was coming back, and with it, all her defensive mechanisms.

Mike mustn't know how silly she'd been!

'I haven't had any lunch.'

'No lunch makes you cry?'

'Tom said it would.'

'Wise, old Tom.'

He somehow had hold of one of her hands in both of his, and had become serious.

'I'm flattered.'

'I feel quite foolish. Tom heard someone had been hurt out here. I . . . we thought it was you, because of you being up all night.'

He let go of her hand with a little squeeze and began teasing her again.

'Which goes to show, one shouldn't take too much notice of gossip. As you can see, I'm alive and well.'

Jennifer wasn't going to point out it wasn't gossip but her imagination that had taken her miles out of her way on a busy afternoon.

'Such devotion by my former employer is a recommendation in itself. Since you haven't eaten and are dressed for town,

I would like to take you to lunch.'

He looked at his watch.

'Hey, it seems lunch is over. Well, it'll have to be sandwiches and coffee in a café. How about it?'

Jennifer remembered Mrs Taylor's parcel. She leaned over into the back seat and brought it out.

'I have the sandwiches,' she said, 'but no coffee.'

'My Thermos is in the truck.'

Mike moved to open the car door. Good sense was telling her this was as good a chance as any to leave.

'Wait!'

She reached out and touched his arm.

'Could I take a raincheck on that? I'm not able to stay. I have to be at Warren's soon. Some other time, perhaps,' she said, knowing it wasn't likely — she would see to that.

Mike nodded and settled back in his seat.

'But you must eat something,' he insisted.

'Just one,' she said, and offered him first choice of the sandwiches. 'I'll ring

Tom from town to let him know you're OK. He and Mrs Taylor were concerned.'

'Do you have a mobile?'

She shook her head.

'I'll do it now, Jennifer. Give me the number.'

He looked at her as he keyed it into his mobile.

'Oh, hello, Tom, it's Mike Manning. Yes, I'm OK. It was poor Wayne. Broke his leg. The good news is it was a clean break so he'll be all right. Yes, she's here with me now. We're eating your wife's sandwiches. I'm glad of them. It's been quite a morning.'

His eyes still held hers, full of double meaning.

'Appreciated your concern, Tom. Goodbye.'

He closed his mobile and began eating.

'I don't remember lamb sandwiches ever tasting so good.'

'That's because you've never had Northwood Park lamb sandwiches with

Mrs Taylor's relish before.'

He took no notice.

'I think it's because I've never had a picnic in the front seat of a BMW.'

'What about in the carpark at the Picnic Races?' she teased.

'Not in the front seat,' he insisted.

They were laughing together again. Jennifer was over her fright and it was just like breakfast had been, but with a difference. Something in the back of her mind was urging her to get out of here. The clock on the instrument panel reminded her of her appointment with Warren. Was that it? She parcelled the remaining sandwiches for Mike.

'You'll have to finish the picnic in the front seat of a truck,' she said and smiled.

'Nothing new about that,' he said as he got out.

Reluctantly, she put her hand to the ignition key and turned it. The engine purred.

'And see you get something to drink in town,' he ordered as she drove away down the drive.

9

Jennifer's smile of goodbye stayed on her face as she drove over the cattle grid and turned the car in the direction of the town. It was all so different to her anxious arrival just an hour ago, she mused. Nothing had happened to Mike! Her lips quivered as the thought of what might have been momentarily shadowed her relief.

He'd been in her life for months as a business friend but her response today certainly had not been that of a mere friend. Somehow, somewhere, she'd crossed the line between friendship and . . . and what?

Like the rewinding of a video tape in slow motion, her mind rolled back over the time she'd known Mike Manning. If she was honest, she'd admit there'd been an attraction between them from the first day they'd met. He'd captured her imagination by his creative ideas for Northwood Park, but had it begun before that? The early glimpse of him, the stranger, playing Judy's piano the night of the party, perhaps? And her feelings had grown. Into what, her inner voice persisted.

The terms of Neil's will meant there could be nothing between them, but Mike obviously cared about her, despite his prejudice against well-to-do widows, and she cared about him. There! It had been admitted. She cared! Was it the end of the world? Of course not.

Jennifer wished she'd taken up his offer of coffee. It might have sorted her muddled thinking. Nothing had changed, that is, if she discounted the truth of their feelings for each other. And what exactly did she mean by caring? More than friendship but not quite love? Or was it love? How could she tell? She'd never been in love.

She'd reached the top of The Gap, the hill overlooking the town. She pulled off the road in the lookout lay-by and turned off the engine, her thoughts switching to her appointment with Warren. He seemed unusually insistent about this meeting. Probably something else to do with the will.

The will! Now that she realised how deeply inolved with Mike she'd allowed herself to become, she needed to pull herself together, to re-set the boundaries. There was no future for them, not without her giving up her inheritance. But the thought of losing Northwood Park had none of the gutwrenching pain she felt when she imagined Mike injured or perhaps killed.

She couldn't believe it! Was it possible she loved him more than she loved the house? A new emotion gripped her. Yes, yes, her heart cried.

★ ★ ★

Jennifer was glad there was no delay in getting to see Warren. She couldn't have waited another minute. The drive into town at the prescribed speed limit had tested her patience.

'Oh, Warren, you won't believe it. I don't myself. I have so much to tell you, and Judy.'

'Jennifer!'

He closed the door behind her and showed her to a chair in front of his desk.

'I've asked Charlene to bring us coffee,' he said.

'Thank goodness. I need one badly. Mike . . .'

With her new awareness her tongue stumbled over his name.

'Mike offered me one but I was running late.'

For the first time she noticed his unusually strained manner.

'What is it, Warren?'

'I don't know how to tell you this.'

He got up and paced the room. Jennifer swivelled in her chair, following Warren's movements, her eyes searching his face. Something there made her shiver with apprehension.

'The accountant,' he began, then

began again. 'David Buckley found details of share-market trading on the Internet on Neil's laptop. He's been able to trace — '

'Share trading?' she interrupted.

That was surprising but hardly serious. Why was Warren making so much of it?

'Neil could have been horse-trading or selling the Sydney Harbour Bridge for all he told me. You know that.'

Warren didn't smile at her attempt at humouring him.

'It wasn't straightforward. He was into dealing, in a big way. In simple terms, he bought options with the idea that the shares would rise in value and he would make a lot of money.'

'And you're telling me that isn't quite a normal activity?'

'Why, no, it's one of the usual trading activities on the Stock Exchange.'

Jennifer was bewildered.

'If it's normal, why hasn't it shown up before this?'

'That's it. He opened a separate

account, in a false name, a nominee company.'

'I don't know much about business, but I didn't think anyone could do that nowadays. Doesn't one need identification?'

'Let's not go down that road. It's not important. The fact is, he did it.'

A cold shiver ran up and down her spine.

'There's more to come, isn't there?' she asked, hoping he would say no.

Warren gave up his restless wandering and sat down behind his desk again. He looked across it at Jennifer.

'Yes, I'm afraid so.'

'And?'

'To fund this account he put up the deeds to Northwood Park to get a loan.'

Jennifer struggled to understand.

'Is that where the Certificate of Title is?'

'Yes, with a finance company known to be a lender of last resort.'

'A lender of last resort? What does that mean?'

'They are a company charging exorbitant interest rates to borrowers who can't or don't want to take out a regular bank loan. Look, you don't need to know all this.'

What did she need to know? It was hard to think of a question that would give her the right answers.

'So we have to pay back the loan, is that it?'

Warren opened a manila folder on his desk, the lines on his face deepening still further, as if the contents pained him.

'It's a little more complicated than that,' he said gravely. 'You see, he used the borrowed funds to invest heavily, very heavily, in a certain stock, gambling on a take-over.'

There was a knock at the door. Charlene entered with a tray. Jennifer welcomed the interruption. It was too much to take in, the talk of shares, options and take-overs quite bewildering. There was silence in the room as each of them thoughtfully sipped their coffee. At last, Warren put his down.

'What he was doing is news to me, you understand. He never mentioned it, although I advised him on all other business matters. I think he knew I wouldn't approve of gambling so much money.'

There was another, even longer pause before he continued.

'The pity is, Neil was spot on. He must have had a tip-off. Probably that was why he kept it secret, rather than risk questions being asked. Anyway, the shares rose dramatically, but by that time he had been killed. Because I didn't know about his dealings, I couldn't act on the options. They lapsed.'

Jennifer tried to beat down the rising suspicion that there was something Warren was still holding back.

'Probate law demands the bequests to the Hetherington brothers be paid, unless they waive their claim on the estate,' he went on.

'That's not likely,' Jennifer interposed

wryly, thinking of the lengths they'd gone to so far in their efforts to gain possession of Northwood Park.

There hadn't been a chance to tell Warren about that.

'Even if they did, neither you nor the estate have the funds to repay this loan. As I said, he borrowed heavily, and the high interest has been accumulating all this time. We couldn't get a second mortgage without the Certificate of Title, and the lender will not give that up until the loan is repaid.'

'And the bottom line is?'

'Northwood Park will have to be sold.'

The telephone was ringing in the empty house when Jennifer returned to Northwood Park. She switched on the light in the hall and glanced at her wristwatch. It was probably her mother. Margaret usually rang about this time each evening now winter had come.

Jennifer wondered how her mother would react to the news. She always expected her daughter would re-marry.

That was why she hadn't come to live at Northwood Park, but neither of them could have imagined Neil's secret share dealings and the fateful result.

It meant Jennifer would be looking for somewhere new to live, and despite their scheming, the Hetherington brothers would be getting no more than their legacy, and be considered lucky at that. She supposed it could be called poetic justice.

She reached for the telephone with one hand and loosened her scarf with the other.

'Jennifer Hetherington!' she announced.

'I'm checking if you finally got that cup of coffee.'

Her breath caught in her throat.

'Mike!' she squeaked.

He picked up on the sound.

'Are you all right?'

Jennifer heard a vehicle door slamming and footsteps on the gravel.

'Yes.'

She dropped the handset back into its cradle and turned. The door had not closed behind her. Mike stood in the light that spilled out on to the veranda, pocketing his mobile phone.

He didn't know it but everything was changed between them. Whatever would she say to him? That she was no longer a woman of means? Would he want to hear that? Now face to face with him, doubt invaded her mind. Had she only imagined he cared? Had he just been flirting and using her money as an excuse? There wasn't time to think about it. He was here.

Jennifer had seen Mike standing at her door before, in all weathers, in all moods, but there was something different about him tonight, something purposeful. She shivered, but not from the cold.

'Come in,' she invited, shrugging herself out of her coat. 'I'll light a fire in the library. It'll be more comfortable in there.'

She didn't wait for him, hurrying down the hallway.

'Don't bother,' he called after her. 'I

thought we might go out for a meal. I owe you one, remember.'

She stopped and turned around. He was still in his overcoat.

'That is, if you would like to,' he went on, his long legs covering the distance between them quickly. 'It's the normal way to go about wooing a woman, I believe.'

Jennifer was having trouble with her voice again.

'Wooing a woman?' she stammered.

His eyes were warm.

'Yes, even though she's a widow with money.'

She had to get this right. Her loveless first marriage had been a terrible mistake. Was she being given a second chance at happiness? Unbelievably, it seemed so.

'Are you saying . . . '

His voice deepened.

'I'm saying I've wanted to woo you from the moment I first saw you.'

Jennifer thought of that first day, of standing in the midst of the whirlwind.

She'd been right — he had wanted to kiss her.

'But I didn't know how long you'd been a widow.'

'And I had money,' she reminded him, emboldened by his words.

'Yes, you had money, and I had a hang-up about rich widows, but today I realised you cared about me, cared enough to race across the countryside to see if I was all right.'

He grinned.

'Instead of just calling me on my mobile.'

The smile left his face.

'I decided nothing should stand between us.'

And suddenly, nothing did. She was in his arms, held tightly against the rough wool of his coat.

'We'll work something out,' he murmured into her hair.

Jennifer's heart was racing. Once, his lips had actually touched the corner of her mouth, promising. Now she lifted her face for the kiss that had been a long time coming. It wasn't a disappointment.

'That was a good start,' she managed to say at last, all wobbly at the knees.

Then, seriously doubting her ability to walk, she made a suggestion.

'Why don't we stay in and talk this through?'

Mike laughed.

'Talk? That's not likely. No, we'll do this the right way. I want the world to know. Grab your coat.'

With his arm about her, she managed to walk toward the still-open front door. The telephone rang as they passed it.

'That'll be my mother,' she told him, reluctantly drawing away from him long enough to lift the receiver and juggle it between her shoulder and ear.

'Hello, Mum.'

Mike kissed her exposed neck and she squirmed with delight.

'Would you mind if I called you back later? I have something to tell you.'

'And I have something to tell you,' she said to Mike Manning as she put down the phone.

'Over dinner,' he insisted, silencing her with another kiss.

But it was a while before Jennifer got around to the telling. They had so many other things to talk about. In the restaurant there were quite a few diners known to them both. Jennifer heard the underlying buzz their appearance excited. She smiled. It wouldn't take long for the news to engulf the town.

A mild panic gripped her. She hadn't told Warren how she felt about Mike. Their meeting had become bogged down in a discussion of details about selling Northwood Park.

'What is it?' Mike asked.

'I just thought of Judy and Warren. I wouldn't want them to hear about this on the bush telegraph.'

'Why don't we ring them?' Mike asked, taking his mobile phone from his pocket.

Jennifer couldn't get used to making calls in public.

'What, now?'

'I'll go outside, if you'd rather. What would you like me to tell them?'

A faint blush warmed her face. She wasn't used to the naked truth in his eyes, either.

'Just tell whoever answers that we're having dinner together.'

'Isn't that a bit prim and proper?'

Like a ghost from the past, a memory crossed her mind of the old Jennifer to whom decorum had been so important, but that Jennifer began disappearing the first day Mike loosened her hair, standing in a dusty paddock in the midst of a whirlwind that swept away her inhibitions. She could see he was remembering, too.

'You were only pretending to be prim and proper, weren't you?' he teased.

She marvelled at his perception. He was so right! Her whole life until now had been a pretence. Without waiting for her reply, he began dialling.

'I thought you were going outside to do that,' she nagged, reluctant to give up all her old ways.

'Stop it,' he ordered softly and passed the tiny phone across the table.

'Judy, it's Jennifer. Mike and I are having dinner at The Chinaman's Hat.'

To her surprise, it wasn't news to Judy.

'Yes, I know.'

'You know? How can you? We just got here!'

'Warren said he met Mike in the street after work. He was all dressed up.'

Jennifer could just imagine what the excitable Judy made of the news of the dinner date. She wondered if Mike had confided his full intentions to Warren. Suddenly who told whom, and what, became too involved.

'Oh, I can't talk now, Judy. Everyone's listening. I'll give you the story tomorrow.'

The mobile was taken from her hand and replaced by the menu.

'That reminds me, what was it you wanted to tell me?' Mike asked.

★　★　★

Jennifer stood at her open bedroom window, gazing out over the green paddocks, now empty of grazing stock. Spring sunlight sparkled off the lake, the thin, smooth leaves of the newly-planted iris at its edge bending slightly in a gentle breeze. Northwood Park had never looked lovelier.

On the steps below her, the auctioneer raised his hand, his eyes searching the crowd.

'For the third and last time . . . '

He turned in the direction of the losing bidder.

'Are you all done, sir? What about another five hundred?'

The man shook his head and turned away. Jennifer was glad. She had her heart set on a younger buyer with a boy balanced on his hip, standing on the outskirts of the large crowd. She'd met him and his family several times during the inspections and liked the idea of them living in her house. The auctioneer called again.

'For the last time . . . going . . . going

. . . gone! Sold to you, sir. Ladies and gentlemen, the new owners of Northwood Park!'

His assistant shepherded the family forward. The young wife with a babe in her arms looked up and mouthed a thank-you to Jennifer before disappearing into the house.

Satisfied with the result, Jennifer turned away from the window to take a last look at herself in the full-length mirror. It reflected her happiness. She was positively radiant. The classic lines of her dress skimmed her figure, the palest-of-pink silk enhancing her lightly-tanned shoulders. Sandals of a deeper shade of pink peeped out from under the hemline.

'Are you ready, Jennifer?' Warren called from the doorway.

'Everything signed?' she asked.

He nodded.

'I've acted on your behalf. But I can't sign the next document.'

She laughed.

'I wouldn't let you,' she replied, joining him.

Her mother was standing at the foot of the stairs as they came down.

'You look lovely, Jenny. Everything in the kitchen is under control. Mrs Taylor's gone to put her hat on.'

Jennifer couldn't help laughing. Mrs Taylor in a hat was something she just had to see. The laugh ended with a tiny sigh. She would miss the Taylors but their retirement to the seaside to be near their daughter was well-earned.

She moved through to the morning-room. Of all the rooms in the house, this was her favourite, and the cats loved it, too, but there was no sign of Boots or Smudge today. The extra people coming and going had sent them scurrying off to secret hiding places in the hay shed. They'd miss the farm life, too, but would soon find their own little nooks and crannies in the new house. Should she say houses? That was to be her future way of life.

'You made Northwood Park a beautiful place but we'll do that again. We're good at it, with other houses,' Mike had said, when she finally told him the news about having to sell up.

'Are you suggesting a partnership without me having to study for a degree?'

'You don't need one for this partnership,' he replied, taking her hands in his. 'You already qualify and it will be for life.'

He had then leaned across the restaurant table, kissing away her doubts.

'Will you marry me?'

The last trace of the old Jennifer disappeared as she gave him her answer and returned his kiss — in public!

Warren's voice brought her back to the present.

'You've come a long way, Jennifer, and done a good job. I'm very happy for you.'

'Dear Warren. You know I couldn't have made it without you.'

She blinked away the sudden tears. He brought out an immaculate handkerchief and dabbed at her cheeks.

'Leaving Northwood Park is not an ending but a beginning,' he said.

They stepped through the french windows and out into the garden. Judy was waiting there to place a circlet of tiny rose-buds on her friend's head and a matching posy in her hand. The garden no longer showed signs of the drought that brought Mike into her life. Bloomer-pots of annuals, a gift from his father and transported from the hot-houses of Adelaide, carpeted the mulched beds with colour. Through an archway dripping with heavily-scented purple wisteria, she could see Mike, tall and dark, waiting for her.

A smattering of applause from the guests alerted him to her approach, his smile deepening as he came to take her hand. The marriage celebrant began to speak.

'Friends, we have gathered here today, in this beautiful garden, to honour these two creative people as they begin a new life together.'

Lost in a dream world, Jennifer

hardly heard the words, conscious only of the man at her side. His grip on her hand tightened.

'I do,' he said.

'And do you, Jennifer, take Michael to be your lawful, wedded husband, to have and to hold for as long as you both shall live?'

Jennifer couldn't think of anything she'd rather agree to.

'I do,' she replied.

The breeze stirred the cherry-plum tree, sending a drift of pink blossom over them as they exchanged rings.

'Then, with the powers vested in me, I now pronounce you man and wife. Michael, you may kiss your bride.'

It was no longer a dream. Mike's arms were about her, his lips against hers, murmuring, 'I love you, Jennifer Manning.'

'And I love you, too,' she said, when she got her breath back.

DIVIDED LOYALTIES

Phyllis Demaine

When Heather's fiancé, Adrian, is offered a wonderful job in America their future seems rosy. However, Adrian's brother, Carl, a widower, asks for Heather's help with his small, deaf son. Help which, as a speech therapist, Heather is qualified to give. But things become complicated when Carl goes abroad on business and returns with Gisel, to whom his son takes an instant dislike. This puts Heather in the position of having to choose between the boy's happiness and her own.

THE PERFECT GENTLEMAN

Liz Pedersen

When Laura agrees to help Anthony Christopher to deceive his family she has no idea how far the web of intrigue will extend, or how it will alter her life. His family is as unpleasant as he promised, but Laura drives away from his funeral thinking she has escaped their malicious clutches. However, this is not so. James Christopher is determined to discover what was behind his cousin's precipitate marriage. He despises Laura and hates the fact that he is attracted to her.